"Are you angry a

"No," he said with a sharp shake of his

But he was.

He turned back to stare at the road. "I'm angry at the situation." His voice was low and even.

"The situation of me trying to help someone?"

"You were reckless." Another glance her way. Softer this time and not so full of reproach. "Brave, too, but reckless. I knew you were gutsy, but had no idea you would go out there with a baseball bat. After you called me, you should've waited inside Delgado's. You could've been seriously hurt—or worse."

If she had been, then it would've put him in a difficult spot with her brother. She hadn't considered the impact her actions might've had on him.

"I didn't mean to make things more difficult for you," she said. During all their discussions, they had never talked about the hard time he was going through. Or the pervasive negative gossip about him that had spread through town like a disease...

WYOMING CHRISTMAS STALKER

Juno Rushdan

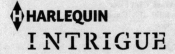

For K.I.R. and A.B.R. Every book I write is for you. Belief fuels
passion, and passion rarely fails. Always follow your dreams.

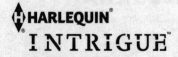

ISBN-13: 978-1-335-58232-4

Wyoming Christmas Stalker

Copyright © 2022 by Juno Rushdan

Recycling programs
for this product may
not exist in your area.

Harlequin Enterprises ULC
22 Adelaide St. West, 41st Floor
Toronto, Ontario M5H 4E3, Canada
www.Harlequin.com

Printed in U.S.A.

Juno Rushdan is the award-winning author of steamy, action-packed romantic thrillers that keep readers on the edge of their seats. She writes about kick-ass heroes and strong heroines fighting for their lives as well as their happily-ever-afters. As a veteran air force intelligence officer, she uses her background supporting Special Forces to craft realistic stories that make readers sweat and swoon. Juno currently lives in the DC area with her patient husband, two rambunctious kids and a spoiled rescue dog. To receive a free book from Juno, sign up for her newsletter at junorushdan.com/mailing-list. Also be sure to follow Juno on BookBub for the latest on sales at bit.ly/bookbubjuno.

Visit the Author Profile page at Harlequin.com.

CAST OF CHARACTERS

Chief Deputy Sheriff Holden Powell—This tough cowboy cop must find a murderer, stop a vicious stalker and protect the one woman he wants but can't have.

Grace Clark—She left sunny California for a fresh start in the Cowboy State of Wyoming where her brother is the sheriff. But after witnessing a murder, a stalker draws closer with her in his sights, and only one man can protect her.

Becca Hammond—An FBI agent working on a local joint task force. She shares Holden's suspicion and interest in the Shining Light cult.

Marshall McCoy—The charming and dangerous cult leader of the Shining Light.

Holly Powell—Holden's mother is a kind but shrewd woman who can't help meddling in her children's lives if she thinks it will bring them happiness.

Chapter One

As Grace Clark closed the lid of the dumpster behind Delgado's Bar & Grill after tossing the night's trash, a woman's shriek rent the air, causing Grace to spin on her heels.

The sound had come from the B and B that sat across the street, catty-corner to the restaurant's parking lot. On the exterior staircase that led to the second-floor rooms stood a tall man wearing a black leather jacket and motorcycle helmet, holding a woman by her arm. Although taller than the average woman, she was inferior in height and weight, making her no match for her assailant. Grace crossed the parking lot behind Delgado's and marched through the snow for a closer look. Her hair whirled around her face, and she pushed the strands behind her ears, the cold December wind a stark reminder that she'd left her coat inside.

In the distance, the sky lit up with a flash of lightning. The air was brittle, almost crackling, and the approaching storm made the night darker and gloomier.

She stopped on the corner, about a hundred feet away from the B and B. The man must have tightened his grip on her arm because the young brunette suddenly winced as she leaned into his grasp. He shouted something at her, but all Grace made out were a few angry curses.

"Hey," Grace called out. "Are you all right?"

The couple glanced her way. The guy's visor was raised but the helmet blocked most of his face. Almost immediately, he swiveled his head away and let the woman go.

A nervous shiver ran down Grace's spine. She had definitely stepped into the middle of something.

Looking relieved, the brunette held her arm against her chest. "Yeah, I'm fine," she said, with a quick wave of her uninjured hand. Her voice was a little shaky and ragged, raw with emotion. Her features were tense, her expression uneasy. She wore a thin quilted jacket and canvas shoes better suited for autumn than the frosty start of winter. "Thanks."

Grace nodded, although she didn't believe her. It was obvious the man was up to no good, but fear had a way of silencing people.

The next flash of lightning was noticeably closer than the first, and a roll of thunder echoed through the air. Grace tilted her head up. A drop of rain hit her cheek as gray clouds roiled. The first time this month the evening temperatures hadn't dipped below freezing and they were going to pay for it with a rainstorm.

Grace eased back toward the restaurant. She didn't want to leave the distressed woman, but she also didn't want to get soaked and catch pneumonia. A California girl, born and raised, she was still acclimating to the Wyoming weather among other things. She had needed a fresh start in every possible way. Job. Landscape. Focus. A total overhaul of her support system.

On a whim, she had decided to pack up and drive across the country to the place that her brother called home. She figured her life couldn't get any more different than in the Cowboy State. Low taxes, unspoiled nature, zero smog, no traffic—a miracle in itself. Besides, the spirit of the Old West was alive and well here and there were actual cowboys. Most people were friendly—the genuine kind, not the SoCal fake kind— and sociable to the point of being gossipy, and hardworking as well. And there was snow, plenty of that. Snakes, too. She could do without both, most especially the latter.

She reached the shelter of the restaurant's overhang just as the sky opened up. Rain pelted the snow still on the ground. Across the way, the couple had moved under the covering at the top of the landing. But now the rain drummed out any other noises and obscured her view.

It concerned Grace that the brunette hadn't used the storm to say a hurried goodbye, get away from him and go inside. As she had made eye contact with the woman, Grace had sensed an inkling of danger. And felt an urgency to help her. Maybe it was because they were both young females. Grace had just turned twenty-five and the other woman looked about the same age, possibly younger. Women had to stick together, especially when one was in a vulnerable position.

Regardless of the reason, she felt an odd connection to her.

Grace traipsed inside the restaurant, needing to close

up and go home, but concern for the woman had her on edge now. It was like one of those dark, ominous clouds, filling the air with anticipation and a palpable dread. Trouble was rolling in along with the storm.

She peeked through the blinds covering the window that offered the best vantage point at the rear of the restaurant to see the B and B. With the deluge, she couldn't see much beyond the parking lot.

Back in Los Angeles when neighbors quarreled, you watched from the security of your living room with a pair of binoculars and a cell phone at the ready to dial 911. She wasn't sure how things were done out here, but her binoculars were in her rented cottage. At night and with the rain, she probably wouldn't be able to see much more if she had them anyway.

Rather than lock up for the night as she had planned to do, she grabbed her coat and the solid wood baseball bat they kept under the bar in case of emergencies. If this had happened two hours earlier, Xavier Triggs would have been there to help. Like her, he poured drinks and served tables. Unlike her, he cared about watching football. She had offered to close on Sundays, Mondays and Thursdays, giving him the chance to enjoy the late game from home with his wife, who also loved the sport. As manager, she didn't have to close at all since she made the schedule, but she did anyway, grateful to Lynn Delgado for having given her the job when she had little experience. Lynn had understood Grace's need for a break from her emotionally demanding job as a nurse in palliative care while she worked on an advanced degree part-time. Now Grace was trying to prove, mostly to herself, that even with online classes she could still be a team player.

On her way to the rear door, she grabbed an umbrella. Pulling her hood up over her head, she pushed on the metal bar of the back door and stepped outside. Heavy rain drummed against the roof. She opened the umbrella and then considered how she was going to wield both that and the bat. If the bat turned out not to be for show and she had to use it, two hands would be required.

Staring at the B and B through the veil of rain, she ditched the umbrella. Water poured off the overhang, splashing the sidewalk in front of her. Soon it would turn the snow into slush ice. Good thing she had taken Lynn's advice by purchasing a pair of Sorel Caribou boots for the winter and packed away her flip-flops and tennis shoes for the foreseeable future.

Lightning splintered the sky in a bright flash. Shadows danced on the landing of the B and B's exterior staircase. The couple was still outside. It was hard to tell whether they were talking or fighting, but she hoped things had simmered down.

She took out her cell and called the sheriff's office.

One of the perks of being the sheriff's sister was she could ask a deputy to do a drive-by, her worry being sufficient reason. Her brother had only been in the job for a little less than a year and he was currently out of town, trying to see if it was possible to reconcile with his ex. Nonetheless, Grace didn't think anyone in the sheriff's department would dismiss her concern.

At least she hoped not.

The call connected. "Chief Deputy Holden Powell."

The sound of his voice, deep and smooth, made her pulse race. Happened every time she heard it and she hadn't gotten used to that feeling. "Hi, it's Grace. I'm calling from Delgado's."

"Is everything okay?" he asked.

"I'm not sure. When I was putting out the trash, I noticed a couple fighting outside the Quenby B and B. I heard her cry out and saw him grab her arm. They're still out there. I'm not sure it's worth disturbing you, but I'm concerned."

"I'll drive by. Take a look. If it turns out to be nothing, I can keep you company while you lock up. Either way, it won't be a wasted trip."

"I'm sorry to trouble you like this."

"No trouble at all," he said, sounding sincere. "See you in a few."

"Thanks." After ending the call, she slipped the phone into her pocket.

Holden would be there soon. But would it be soon enough?

She was aware how easily and quickly a situation could get out of hand. Within minutes. Sometimes it only took seconds. Heck, things could go wrong in a heartbeat.

She needed to buy time without endangering herself. She had the training to handle her own, but you never knew if someone had a gun. It was safest to assume that everyone was carrying.

All she had to do was go over to the B and B and if they were still arguing, share the fact that the sheriff's department was on the way. If it came to that, hopefully that'd be enough to scare the guy, and he'd take off.

Taking a deep breath, she ventured into the downpour and stepped into the parking lot. She nearly slipped right on her backside and had to pinwheel her arms to catch her balance. Grabbing a hold of the side mirror of her vehicle, she made certain that slippery patch wouldn't get her again.

The rain had turned everything into a slick mess quicker than she had expected.

She righted herself, letting the spike in her pulse settle, and trod with more care across the parking lot.

Another bolt of lightning highlighted the couple. The woman tried to open the side door to the B and B on the second floor, but the man slammed it closed before she made it inside.

Rain pounded the pavement. A crack of thunder made Grace jump, but she didn't slow down. Holding the bat with both hands, she hurried to make her presence known over the loud clatter of rain, her anxiety increasing with each step.

She decided to get only as close as necessary so that she could be heard.

As she started across the street, another jagged flare of lightning lit up the B and B. The two were grappling at the top of the landing. The man's hands were locked around her throat, and the woman struggled to get free of his grasp.

Then darkness fell again. Thunder rumbled, so loud now it sounded as if it were overhead. Grace picked up her pace, splashing down the asphalt of the street. A sharp sound pierced the rain-drenched darkness. What was that? A scream?

It was hard to tell over the thrumming rain.

She was close enough now to see the staircase clearly. The guy raced down the steps, hopped onto his motorcycle and cranked the engine.

Lightning forked in the sky.

In the glaring bright flash, Grace spotted the woman, immobile, lying facedown on the pavement near the bottom of the stairs.

Shock paralyzed Grace. Heartbeat skyrocketing, she stood frozen, her gaze riveted to the body that had been animated, struggling only seconds ago.

Her stomach clenched. This was her fault for not acting faster. As soon as she suspected the woman was in trouble, she should have called Holden and come straight over instead of dithering and debating.

High beams flipped on, forcing Grace to squint against the harsh light. She raised a hand, shielding her eyes, but she couldn't see anything through the bright glare. The engine revved and the motorcycle took off, roaring down the street. By the sound, it was headed straight for her, as if to run her down.

A quick punch of fear and dread flooded her veins.

The motorcycle's growl grew louder, the blinding light beaming down on her.

Pulse hammering in her ears, Grace lunged to the side to get out of the way. A split second too late. The bike clipped her, knocking her off her feet, sending her crashing into a parked truck.

Her head slammed against metal. The world spun and blurred. A haze of red and blue flashing lights filled her vision before darkness engulfed her.

Chapter Two

"Grace," Holden said, hunched over her while the EMTs raised the gurney from the ground to waist height, locking the legs. He clasped her cold hand as paramedics wheeled her to the ambulance. "Grace."

Please open your eyes.

As though she could hear his thoughts, her head rocked from side to side and she opened her eyes. It took her a few seconds to focus on him. "Holden? What happened?"

That was what he wanted to know. "You were knocked unconscious. Who did this to you?"

"A man on a motorcycle hit me with his bike," she said weakly, and he'd heard one racing away as he pulled up. "He was fighting with the woman."

"Did you see his license plate? Did you get a good look at him?"

"No, uh, I didn't." She glanced around. "Where are they taking me?"

"An ambulance is here. The paramedics are going to take you to the hospital and make sure you're okay."

"No." She shook her head. "I'm fine."

Grace didn't look it. Her eyes, usually bright and sparkling, were weary. Her golden, tawny-brown skin was pale, and every inch of her was shaking. "You're not fine. You're going to the hospital."

"But I need to check on her. The woman I told you about." Concern tightened her delicate features. "I think she's hurt."

The woman was beyond anyone's help now. After Holden had made sure Grace was alive and radioed for an ambulance, he'd noticed the body and had checked on the woman. No pulse. But he didn't want to burden Grace with that news just yet.

"Don't worry about anything. I've got it under control. You need to go to the hospital. Make sure you don't have a concussion or internal bleeding, or something. We need to be sure you're all right."

Sheriff Daniel Clark had tasked him with two priorities while he was on vacation. Make sure that all hell didn't break loose in town and keep an eye on his little sister.

And by "keep an eye on" he meant "don't let her get into trouble." Apparently, it was too late for that.

Her brother—*his boss*—would never forgive him if she wasn't going to be okay. Holden wouldn't forgive himself, either.

The EMTs needed to get the gurney in the ambulance, so he let go of her hand.

Her soft brown eyes met his and he clenched his jaw against the sudden tug inside him. That happened with her. *A lot.* Sometimes when their eyes met, like now.

Sometimes her smile triggered it. Sometimes it was for no reason at all other than he was near her.

Don't go there. Torturing himself by wanting a woman that he couldn't have would be a huge mistake. Gargantuan.

Holden forced himself to detach, putting space between them on more than one level as he took a step back. "Have a nurse let me know when they have her test results," he said to one of the EMTs. Someone from the hospital would call the sheriff's office and dispatch would relay the message to him.

"Sure thing," the EMT said with a nod before closing the doors.

Shortly thereafter, the ambulance pulled off.

On his way to the crime scene, Holden reached the spot where he'd found Grace unconscious in the street. Anger burned through him. Also fear. Grace could've been killed tonight, on his watch. Whoever did this was going to pay.

He picked up a baseball bat. The letters DBG had been burned into the wood. It was the bat they kept under the bar at Delgado's.

One plus one equaled Grace had been impatient and had acted hastily. Probably driven by a need to be a Good Samaritan albeit an impulsive one.

He hoped she was going to be okay. If he had known she had planned to take matters into her own hands, he would've insisted that she sit tight and wait for him.

Turning, he glanced at the silver truck she'd been lying next to. The right side was scratched like it had been grazed by another vehicle. Perhaps the motorcycle that had hit Grace. He took out his flashlight and looked closer at the front corner. Flecks of black paint were in the grooves.

On the chance that the damage had occurred tonight, he got an evidence bag and scraped the paint flakes inside. Then he sealed it.

A few feet away, the area around the body and the staircase was cordoned off thanks to Deputy Ashley Russo.

"We need to track down the owner of that vehicle." Holden pointed to the truck. "The motorcycle that hit Grace might've scraped it."

"Got it," Ashley said, writing down the plate number.

Glancing up at the second floor of the B and B, Holden swept his flashlight over the landing where the wood railing had been broken as the woman fell to her death.

Or had been pushed.

They wouldn't know for certain until the medical examiner issued a report.

The deceased woman's torso was on the pavement, a stream of blood flowing from her head down the sidewalk into the gutter. The lower half of her body was in the grass. He crouched down next to her, balancing on the balls of his feet. Ten years as a deputy sheriff had toughened him, given him a cold, cynical perspective of death and its many causes. Scenes such as this one no longer shocked, but it continued to sicken him. He looked over the woman. Long brown hair. Brown eyes wide and still with that eerie expression death left behind. Slim build. Early to midtwenties.

The girl had barely lived before her life had ended.

"Do you recognize her?" Ashley asked.

She looked familiar, but her name didn't come to mind. "No." He took in her lightweight jacket and canvas shoes that were worthless in the snow. All odd for this time of year. No purse.

"Did you check her pockets for an ID?" he asked.

"Yes, sir. No such luck. No wallet. No money. Only a set of keys to the B and B." Wearing latex gloves, Ashley handed him the keys.

He donned a set himself before taking them. One key was marked for the exterior door. The other was to room number three. "I'll go take a look around her room. Hang on to that," he said, handing her the baseball bat.

She took it and offered him a couple of evidence bags in return.

"I've got some," he said.

"I already notified the medical examiner. He's on his way. I can start processing the scene if you'd like."

Holden was grateful to have a young deputy who took initiative and didn't have to be told what to do every step of the way. "That would be good. Go ahead."

The ME was on the brink of retiring and was a bit slow responding to calls after dinner. With Ashley handling this end, it freed him up to focus on other things.

He ducked under the yellow crime scene tape. Along the way up the staircase, he swept his flashlight over the steps, keeping his eyes peeled for any evidence. At such times, which thankfully weren't often, he wished that his department had a proper crime scene unit. But they didn't have the manpower or resources. They would have to process the scene themselves and the rain would only complicate the situation.

He checked the exterior door. It was locked. Using the key, he opened the door and stepped into the hall. Two wall sconces were on, providing soft amber light. He shook off a bit of the rain and the cold.

Two doors down he found room number three. Inside the tiny space was a full-size bed that was meticulously made, a nightstand, small armoire and an attached three-piece bathroom. The room was tidy, nothing out of place.

Both the armoire and nightstand were empty, except for a Bible—the inside of the front flap was labeled as the property of the B and B. No clothes were hanging up. No luggage or an overnight bag. Nothing was stowed under the bed or hidden beneath the mattress. A single towel hung from the back of the bathroom door. On the countertop, beside a cheap toothbrush and little dish of what appeared to be homemade toothpaste was a photograph.

Of a little girl.

Maybe three or four years old. The child was smiling and hugging a doll that looked as if it had been made by hand. Yarn for hair. Pieces of felt for eyes. Lips and a rosy hue to the cheeks painted on.

The Polaroid picture was propped up on the mirror. It was in excellent condition. Looked as if it had been taken recently. The photo of the child was the sole personal possession in the room.

Disappointed there wasn't more to go on, Holden bagged the picture.

By the time he went back outside, the rain had stopped, and the medical examiner had arrived and gotten to work. He exchanged a few perfunctory words with the ME, preferring to have an in-depth conversation once he had determined the official cause of death.

"Did you find anything?" Ashley asked.

Holden held up the evidence bag. "That's it. Nothing else."

"I'll take it in and log it. Now what?"

"Time to wake up Mr. and Mrs. Quenby." He could have gone through the house down to the first floor. The owners were used to guests disturbing them at all hours for a variety of reasons, but he didn't want to track rain and mud throughout the place.

At the front of the B and B, he rapped a fist against the door. It was almost eleven forty-five. The owners were surely in bed and would need a minute or two to gather themselves.

He turned on his heel and scanned the area. The back of Delgado's was lit up. Holden could see the rear door, the dumpster and Grace's car parked near Mitch Cody's. He was another deputy, who lived right above the restaurant. When Holden had been waiting for the ambulance, he had called him to see if was still awake. Deputy Livingston was manning the office and there was no one else on duty tonight to assist. Fortunately, Mitch hadn't been asleep and volunteered to come over before Holden could ask despite the fact he was working the early shift. Holden wanted someone in the office he trusted to handle anything that popped up when he was getting shut-eye.

Normally Holden worked from nine a.m. to seven p.m., four days a week unless he was needed. The rest of the time he spent helping out at his family's ranch.

While he was in charge, he had been putting in thirteen-hour days, from eleven in the morning until midnight. Not coincidentally the same hours Grace worked at the bar and grill. On the evenings she closed, he had taken to driving by Delgado's about fifteen minutes to twelve to put his mind at ease that she'd locked up safely.

It wasn't some sixth sense that had compelled him to check on her, only paranoia.

After the disaster that had ruined his life and nearly ended his career last year, *Paranoid* had become his middle name.

A shuffling sound drawing closer on the other side of the door had Holden turning around. The chain slid off and the dead bolt flipped.

All right, Jane Doe, let's find out who you are.

A lanky man with glasses and a receding gray hairline opened the door wearing a robe tied closed over his pajamas. "Holden?" Arthur Quenby looked him over from head to toe. "You're still with the sheriff's department? I thought you were fired."

Unease slithered through Holden. "No, Mr. Quenby. I'm still chief deputy. Because I didn't break the law."

But he had been a naive sucker who had been duped by his former boss and ex-fiancée. The two criminals had conspired and colluded and conned Holden into believing everything was peachy when in fact things had been rotten to the core.

Shame was the gift that kept on giving.

"Huh. I'm surprised they kept you on after everything that happened," Mr. Quenby said, and Holden was sick of folks giving him the "guilt by association" treatment. "I suppose it's because you're a Powell."

Gritting his teeth, Holden ignored the comment. "Mr. Quenby, I need to ask you a few questions about one of your guests."

"Would you like to step inside?"

"No, thank you." He didn't see the need to get the Quenbys' foyer wet. "Did you have a guest staying in room number three?"

"Not *did*, I do. Why? Did she get into some kind of trouble?"

"What was her name?"

"Skye. Why do you keep using the past tense?"

This part was never easy. Always harder when you had to notify the family, but telling someone that there was a dead body on their premises wasn't pleasant, either. "We found her body on your property. At the foot of the exterior staircase that leads to the second-floor rooms."

"Body? She's dead?"

Giving a slight nod, Holden asked, "Do you happen to have a surname for Skye?"

"Starlight. Skye Starlight."

Holden groaned. That wasn't her real last name. But he knew where to go to find out. The same place where all the other Starlights lived.

"She was from that compound," Mr. Quenby said, quirking an eyebrow.

It was as though the words had been plucked from Holden's mind.

Once again, Holden nodded, dreading that he would have to step inside the infamous compound of the Shining Light cult. Led by Marshall McCoy, who now went by Empyrean, but he hadn't made the name a legal change.

"Figured as much," Holden said.

"I wonder what goes on in there, what it's like."

Holden didn't. "How long was she here?"

"This was her third day. She had to go back tomorrow."

"Did she say why she *had* to leave? Was someone forcing her to go?"

"I don't know." Arthur lifted his shoulder. "Something about the phases of the moon."

"Of course," Holden grumbled and restrained a sigh. Everything regarding those cultists revolved around the lunar cycles. "How did she pay for the room? Did she use a credit card? Cash?"

"Credit card?" Arthur scoffed. "She barely had adequate clothes and didn't have any money. Claimed her 'secular family,'" he said, using air quotes, "wouldn't let her stay with them this time, but she was willing to work to cover the cost of the room. Mildred and I took pity on her. We had her clean the bathrooms, do laundry, as well as change the linen in the other room being occupied."

"Who else is staying with you?"

"A fellow from out of town, a Mr. Hughes, visiting family in the area for the holidays. Quiet. Keeps to himself."

"Did Skye happen to mention her birth family's surname or where they live?"

Arthur shook his head. "Nope."

Great. "Was this her first time staying with you?" Holden asked.

"Yup, it sure was."

"To your knowledge, did she have any visitors? Receive any phone calls?"

Arthur mused the question a moment and then shook his head. "Not that I'm aware of. She was quite friendly, but not too talkative. A nice girl. Hard worker. Such a shame." The older man rubbed at his salt-and-pepper beard. "How did she die?"

"I'm not at liberty to discuss details of an ongoing investigation," Holden said.

"Oh, all right." Arthur's tone rose in surprise as he tightened his robe's belt. "I was just curious."

"That's all the questions I have for now." Holden's cell phone rang. He fished it out of his pocket and glanced at the screen. The number was to the hospital. "Deputy Russo will come in, get a statement from the other guest and secure the entrance. Mr. Hughes will have to use the front door for a few days. Excuse me, I have to take this. Try to get some sleep, Mr. Quenby." Walking away, he answered. "Chief Deputy Powell."

"Hi, this is Terri Tipton over at Laramie General."

He knew her. They had gone to high school together, though Terri had been two grades ahead of him. "How is Grace?"

"We ran a CT scan. It looks good and the doctor said no concussion. She's going to be fine," Terri said, and Holden exhaled a small breath of relief. "We're not going to admit her, but she'll need a ride home."

"Okay. Thanks. Let her know that someone will be there shortly," he said, hoping that person would be him, but he needed to check on the crime scene first. Putting away his phone, he made a beeline to Ashley. "Hey, do you think you can handle this for about an hour? Get a statement from the other guest once Mitch gets here?"

"Yeah, sure." She put her hands on her hips. "Where are you taking off to?"

"The hospital just called about Grace."

"Is she going to be all right?"

"She got a clean bill of health."

"That's fortunate. You dodged a bullet," Ashley said. "I would've hated to be in your shoes if something happened to her."

His situation at the sheriff's department was already tenuous. He was lucky to have a job and the whole town knew it. Gossip about the scandal still hadn't died down. Likely never would. "I'm going to pick her up and give her a ride home."

"Did we get a name on Jane Doe?"

"Skye. Starlight."

Ashley winced, understanding what it meant. "Are you going to go to the compound?"

Looked as though he had no other choice. "Sometime tomorrow." After he spoke with Special Agent Becca Hammond. She was one of two FBI agents working on a local task force. The other was his best friend, Nash

Garner. His buddy was also on vacation, in Colorado for the holidays with the love of his life, Lynn Delgado.

According to Nash, Becca was the expert on the Shining Light.

"Can I tag along?" Ashley asked. "I've always wanted to see inside that place."

Most folks had that same burning curiosity. Holden was not most folks. He would be happy to never set foot inside the compound.

"Yeah, you can come. Why not?" Besides, he owed her one. "Did you happen to see beneath her jacket, what she was wearing?"

"A knit sweater."

"What color?"

"Green. Why?"

At the moment it wasn't important. Tomorrow, during the visit at the compound, it might matter. The cult had a color system. Each hue meant something different. "Wanted to know for my report. Come to think of it, I didn't notice her wearing one of the Shining Light necklaces." Every member wore one. A pendant of a half-moon and sun. "Did you see one?"

Ashley bent down and took a look. "No necklace. I'll search in the grass and on the landing for it." She stood up. "Do you want me to play chauffeur and save you the hassle of driving Grace home?"

It was no hassle. After finding her unconscious, he needed to see for himself that she was indeed okay. There was also the fact that he enjoyed the moments he got to spend with her, as few and far between as they might be.

"No, I'll do it." He headed for his vehicle, one of the department's SUVs, and spotted Mitch making his way over. "I'll be back as soon as I can."

"Sure you don't want to head home after you drop her off? You need to get some sleep," she called out after him.

He'd love nothing more than that. Long days and long hours were nothing new to him—working a ranch required it—but something told him he was going to need all his strength for this investigation.

"I've got a crime scene to process, a report to file and a job to do," he said. "Sleep will have to wait."

Never in his life had he been a slacker or cut corners, and now more than ever he had a lot to prove. To everyone. Because they were all watching him.

Waiting for him to slip up and fail.

Chapter Three

Grace sat in the emergency waiting room, facing the doors that overlooked the parking lot. They had given her a thorough examination, including a CT scan, and discharged her. She was absolutely mortified. Requiring an ambulance, having people fret about her, taking up their time and energy. She hated being the center of attention.

The spotlight always highlighted things she didn't want others to see.

Now, to compound her shame, Grace was waiting on someone from the sheriff's department to come collect her because they didn't think she was fit to call a cab. Rather than serving as her personal taxi service, the deputies had to actually serve and protect. They had an important job. Holden most of all, while her brother was out of town.

Before she realized what she was doing she had fished out her cell phone and hit the first number saved on speed dial. "Mom."

"Bug, I was just thinking about you, hoping you'd

finally call me. But I sensed something was off with your energy. Are you okay?"

"Um... I..." As the words failed to come to her, she trailed off, not sure how to tell her estranged mother what had happened. Wearing a pair of sweats that a kind nurse had loaned her, Grace was kicking herself for messing up. Yet again. This time it was something as basic as helping someone. She had no idea if that woman was okay, and in the process of trying to avert a tragedy she had only made things worse by getting hurt. Her mother would have scared that guy off with a few choice words, without bothering the police or wielding a bat, and wouldn't have even chipped a nail. "I'm fine."

Her mother gave a prolonged, exaggerated sigh. "Thank heavens." Then her sweet tone soured. "What did you do? I told your brother to keep you out of trouble."

Grace cringed on the inside, realizing her mistake in thinking calling her mom was a good idea. It had been an impulse—a misplaced one—driven out of a desperate need for comfort. "Why do you assume I'm in trouble?"

Melodic laughter rang on the end of the phone. "Bug, darling, you're a veritable lodestone for trouble."

Grace bent over and dropped her head into her hand as her mother, the paragon of perfection, prattled on and on.

Selene Beauvais had once been a model. Not a rail-thin, sickly-looking waif with nothing but legs that went on for miles. Oh, no. Her mother had been a *glamazon*. To this day, she was the epitome of beauty and poise, *with* legs that went on for miles, curves that never failed to turn heads, and an arsenal of killer dresses for a wardrobe. Grace had been blessed with the ability to eat what she wanted without worrying about her weight, but her slender frame looked deflated beside va-va-voom curves. She was cute, perhaps even pretty, but far from being a knockout. As for poise and elegance, well, they had clearly skipped a generation.

Her mother had told her how she had prayed for a daughter who would embody the same qualities as her. But in the end she supposed her mom had to settle for one simply *named* Grace.

Once Selene had discovered her mistake in the choice of names, she took to calling her Love Bug. Somewhere along the way, *love* had been forgotten.

"My worst fear, Bug," her mother said, "is that your life will go through the meat grinder out there in the wilderness. You belong in LA, with the sunshine and *with me*. The weather can be so harsh in Wyoming, as I'm sure you're learning the hard way. I hope you're moisturizing," Selene said as a prelude to launch into Grace's inadequacies. "Please tell me you aren't running around without bothering to put your face on. Remember you represent this family."

Which meant Grace represented her mother. "I like to let my skin breathe."

She also preferred to have her hair loose or in a ponytail, not runway ready. Five-five to her mother's lissome six-one, she never bothered with high heels.

Another sin in the book of Selene.

Her mother tsked. "My advice is to smother those pores in a little makeup. It'll be easier to find a husband. Speaking of which, Kevin told me you haven't been returning his phone calls. I think he wants you back. Call him. Better yet, see him."

"I don't want to talk to Kevin," Grace said. "Or see him." Much less get back together with him. Why was he even calling? She'd been living in Laramie for six months without a peep from him until recently, when the holiday blues rolled around for those who were single.

"Don't you want to see *me*? I think it's time to put an end to this Wild West madness and come home."

It wasn't madness for Daniel, who had moved here to claim his inheritance—a small ranch thirty minutes from downtown. Only for her. The oopsie child their father never knew about and had bequeathed nothing to because he'd passed away shortly after she'd been conceived.

"This is my home now, Mom."

"Oh, that's pishposh. In the morning, I'll book a ticket for you."

As usual, her mother was only listening to herself. "Please, don't buy a ticket. I won't use it." She was determined to stay and build a new life for herself. "I'm not coming back."

"You will. Mark my words," her mother said, and Grace gritted her teeth. "May as well make it sooner rather than later. Stop being so stubborn. I'll email you an e-ticket and we can spend Christmas together. Daniel's not there, right? You don't want to be alone for the holidays, do you?"

No, she didn't. But she also didn't want to spend it in her mother's frosty shadow, constantly being reminded why Selene didn't think she was good enough.

Grace would rather be alone for the rest of her life than live under her mother's thumb another second.

"So I'll get the ticket," her mother said. "First class. My treat."

"*No.* Really, Mom, don't book a flight for me. I'm *never* going back to Los Angeles." Saying the words aloud and meaning them filled her with equal parts euphoria and guilt.

Guilt for having broken free, for being, at last, her own woman, able to live her life on her terms. The remorse was residue—debris—from the hold Selene had once had over her.

But no longer.

My soul is mine again.

Movement outside the doors made Grace lift her head. A sheriff's SUV pulled up under the awning in front of the glass doors of the emergency room.

"I've gotta go, Mom."

"Promise me you'll answer the phone the next time I call, Bug."

In addition to avoiding Kevin's calls, she hadn't taken her mother's, either. Since Grace had been the one to break the moratorium of silence it only seemed fair that she had to live with the consequences. "Promise. Love you. Bye."

Hanging up, Grace gathered her things that were in a plastic bag and hurried to the door, not wanting whichever deputy had been tasked with taxi duty to wait any longer than necessary.

Part of her hoped it wasn't Holden driving, wasting his valuable time like this on her.

The other part of her hoped it was him.

Every time she saw him, he was so nice to her. She'd dare even say sweet. Whenever he came into Delgado's for dinner with his friends, he always ate at the bar and chatted with her until she'd forget she had a job to do. Sometimes he would swing in by himself for a piece of pie and cup of coffee. If it wasn't too busy and she could take a break, he'd offer to buy her a slice on the condition she kept him company. She looked forward to his visits. He spoon-fed her his attention and she happily ate it up. Even though the only reason he went out of his way to be so friendly to her was because he wanted to stay on her brother's good side.

Not that it mattered. She had soured on dating after her breakup with Kevin.

Before the automatic doors whooshed open, Holden was out of the vehicle and standing at the entrance. She looked up into his face and her breath caught in her throat.

"Glad to see you're okay," he said, his voice soothing her frazzled nerves. The corner of his mouth lifted, showing one of his dimples.

It was a small, subtle grin. The gleam in his sky blue eyes was slight. Yet it did strange things to her insides, somehow turning the dreadful churning in her belly into something lighter, warmer.

Holden put his hand on her lower back, guiding her to the vehicle. It was a casual touch, but she was aware of the weight of his hand, of its warmth, of its closeness. Any time he'd touched her before it had been in a playful manner, or accidental. Always brief.

This was different. Something about the lingering contact made her nervous.

Then he opened the passenger door for her and as his hand left her back to help her into the SUV, she missed the feel of it.

He closed the door. A moment later, he was behind the wheel, navigating out of the hospital parking lot. Her cottage wasn't far, only a few miles outside of town.

"Thanks for driving me," she said. "I'm sorry you had to come out to get me. I could've gotten a rideshare or something."

"I wanted to make sure you got home safely. After what you went through tonight, your brother would have my hide if I let you take a cab."

Of course Daniel would. Holden was just being a cautious chief deputy, trying to keep his new boss happy by driving her. Nothing more.

The truth stung.

But she shook it off. "I can't go home yet. I need to lock up the bar and grill."

"Lynn gave me her spare set of keys to the place while she's on vacation with Nash. I can do it for you."

"What about my car?" she asked. "I need it to get to work tomorrow."

"I'll pick you up. You usually leave to head over around ten thirty, don't you?"

"Yeah, I do. How did you know that?"

"Estimated since I've seen you hauling pies from the pastry shop down the block to Delgado's before you open," he said. "I'll be here at ten so I can take your statement at the office first and then drop you."

"But it's really not necessary. If you drop me at the restaurant now, I can spare you the drive tomorrow."

"No buts. You were knocked unconscious. I'm not letting you drive tonight."

He probably thought she was a pain in the neck at this point.

"I'm sorry to be such a bother." More like a burden. She'd have to find some way to make it up to him. Maybe try baking him a pie herself. "How is the woman from the B and B? I asked if she had been brought into the hospital also. Nurse Tipton said she couldn't give me any information about other patients. Is she all right?"

Holden stiffened, his hands tightening on the steering wheel. "When I got to her, she was dead. The medical examiner is at the crime scene now."

Dead. Grace's heart sank. "Was she strangled?"

He gave her a hard glance. "Why would you ask that? Did you see him choking her?"

"I think so." Grace tried to recall exactly what she had seen. The two wrestling. His hands on her. Possibly wrapped around her throat. The woman fighting to get free. "If only I had been faster getting out there."

She had hesitated before as well as after calling the sheriff's department. That delay had cost someone their life.

"Then you might be dead, too," Holden snapped. His gaze, stark and blue and unfathomable, met hers.

Something in her chest tightened uncomfortably. "Are you angry at me?"

"No," he said with a sharp shake of his head.

But he was.

He turned back to stare at the road. "I'm angry at the situation." His voice was low and even.

"The situation of me trying to help someone?"

"You were reckless." Another glance her way. Softer this time. Not so full of reproach. "Brave, too, but reckless. I knew you were gutsy—just had no idea you would go out there with a baseball bat. After you called me, you should've waited inside Delgado's. You could've been seriously hurt. Or worse."

If she had been, then it would've put him in a difficult spot with her brother. She hadn't considered the impact her actions might've had on him.

"I didn't mean to make things more difficult for you," she said. During all their discussions, they had never talked about the hard time he was going through. Or the pervasive negative gossip about him that had spread through town like a disease.

Daniel had shared scant details regarding Holden. She had heard plenty while working at Delgado's to fill in the blanks. Not only had the previous sheriff been involved in some sex trafficking ring, but so had a former judge *and* Holden's fiancée at the time, a parole officer. No one in town believed it was possible that Holden hadn't known. That the chief deputy had had the wool pulled over his eyes by the two people he'd been closest to.

Except for Daniel, who had enough healthy skepticism to let Holden keep his job unless his actions showed that he deserved to be fired. Her brother was a big believer in giving people the benefit of the doubt.

So was Grace. "I understand the position you're in

at the sheriff's department," she said. How precarious things were for him. Daniel was giving Holden a chance, but that didn't erase all of her brother's uncertainty.

"You don't understand what it's like. The cold stares. The snide comments. No one does. One minute I was living a charmed life and just like that—" he snapped his fingers "—it was all snatched away."

It was true. She had never been at the center of a scandal, but she was familiar with the scorching heat of being under a bright spotlight. "I do know what it's like to be underestimated. To be unfairly judged. It's not exactly the same, but I have some idea. I get that it's been hard for you." Glancing down at his hand on the console between them, she wanted to reach out and take it in hers. Instead, she looked out the window. "My brother never should've made me your obligation." Adding her to his list of worries. "I'm sorry about that. I'm a grown woman, responsible for my own actions. I'll call Daniel and ask him to let you off the hook." Assigning Holden as her babysitter wasn't right to either of them.

"Please, stop apologizing."

"What?"

"You apologize a lot. Too much. You shouldn't," he said, his voice still low, thrillingly rough. "There's no need."

She swallowed hard, wondering if he was correct. Did she apologize a lot?

Holden turned down the long rural road that her cottage was on. The houses and ranches were spread far apart with a mile or more of land between them. To her, the road was too dark, needing more lampposts, and the area felt somewhat isolated. Lonely. Not to mention she disliked the fact that it was dirt and gravel, forcing her to drive under thirty-five miles per hour on it.

"Your brother did the right thing," Holden said. "And I'm fine staying on *this* hook."

"Daniel thinks you're a good deputy." She tilted her head at him, peering closer, and captured a glimpse from him. "It won't hurt your standing with him at the department if I spoke to him. You don't need to worry about that. I'll make sure of it. Your job is safe. Really."

Holden turned into her driveway and parked in front of the quaint cottage she called home.

She grabbed the door handle to get out.

"Hey." He put a gentle hand on her shoulder, drawing her gaze, and leaned in. "You're new in town. No family here besides Daniel. No friends from what I can tell. You need someone to look out for you, someone you can turn to for whatever reason. I don't mind being that person and it's not because I'm worried about my job," he said, giving her *the look*—a torturous mix of sincerity and sweet heat.

She wasn't sure if the heat on his part was real or if she was imagining it, but what was undeniable was the flutter of butterflies in her belly whenever she was the focus of his attention.

His gaze slipped to her mouth, and for a second she thought he might lean closer. Might even kiss her.

But did she want him to?

In that heartbeat of her uncertainty, Holden lowered his head along with his hand, dropping it from her shoulder. "Everyone needs a friend that they can count on."

Her attraction to him might be one-sided, which was honestly for the best, but at least their budding friendship wasn't.

"Thanks for the ride." She opened the door.

"If you need anything else tonight, give me a call. Regardless of the hour."

"Are you working all night?"

His brow furrowed. "No. I'll text you. So you have my cell number. Call anytime."

Guess that meant he already had hers. "Okay," she said with no intention of disturbing him any more tonight. No matter what.

"I'll wait until you get inside."

Seemed like overkill, but she wasn't going to fight him on it.

She hopped out, shutting the door behind her. She climbed the four steps up to the porch and dug out her keys from her coat pocket. A little tremor of awareness went through her as she felt him watching her while she unlocked the door. She liked it.

Grace gave a quick wave. He returned it. She ducked inside and locked the door as he drove off.

By the time she was sliding the chain on, her cell phone dinged. She took it out and the phone slipped through her fumbling fingers, but she managed to catch it before it hit the floor.

Hey, this is Holden. Get some sleep.

She pulled back the curtain. Watching him drive away on the road, she texted him.

You, too. Thanks again. For everything.

Holden: You're welcome. And FYI, you're not a bother to me.

Biting her lower lip, she stared at the words, not wanting to read more into them. Better to take it at face value. Looking at his last text once again, she couldn't help but smile.

The friend zone was safe. But it didn't mean a girl couldn't fantasize. And Holden gave her plenty to imagine.

High cheekbones. Classically handsome chiseled features. Adorable dimples. Sunny blond hair. Startling blue eyes. Tanned skin. And his body... The thought of it made her tingle.

He was so hot. In that riding-horses, hands-dirty, bailing-hay, well-worn-jeans way. In addition to being the chief deputy, he was a rancher.

One thing was for certain, he had hit pay dirt when it came to his looks, and he had an air of confidence that made him even more attractive.

Still smiling, she flipped the switch, turning on the light in the living room along with the Christmas tree.

"Evening, Grace."

Gasping, she stopped dead, her belongings falling from her hands as her skin coated in ice when she heard a deep male voice that shouldn't be coming from her living room. She stared at the burly man stretched out on the recliner with his feet up, facing her.

Rodney Owens.

Air stuck in her lungs.

He was skulking in the darkness like a predator to scare her senseless, and it was working because she didn't know what he was capable of, and *he was in her living room*!

"What are you doing in my house?" Her heart hammered in her throat. "It's after midnight."

"Not like you keep banker's hours." He grinned. The look was feral. "And this is my house."

Technically, the house belonged to Oscar Owens, his father.

"I'm a tenant who pays rent. That makes this my home." Fighting against the trembling of her body, she folded her arms across her chest and squared her shoulders, refusing to let this creep see how much he was frightening her. "You can't just come in here whenever you want. Legally you have to give me notice." Even then, he shouldn't be waiting for her in the dark like some weirdo.

"I didn't have to give you notice," he said.

"I'm no lawyer, but I know my rights."

Pulling the lever on the side of the chair, he lowered his feet to the floor. He bent over and picked up a toolbox. Wearing jeans, a dark jacket and work boots, he crossed the open space and came right up to her. His hair was as greasy and slick as the smile spreading wider over his face. "Might want to check those rights again," he said, looming over her. "You requested maintenance. I fixed your water heater."

That part was good. The rest was unacceptable. "Why didn't you leave after you were finished?"

"Because I wanted a word with you."

This was exactly what she *didn't* need after the night she'd had. Whenever Rodney spoke to her it was always about one thing.

Grace groaned. "Not now."

"I want you out of here come the new year," he said, ignoring her.

"That's going to be a problem, considering my one-year lease isn't up until June."

"My father promised to sell this parcel of land and the house along with it. I was counting on that money and I intend to get it."

Oscar had almost reached his breaking point, on the verge of caving in to Rodney's demands to sell this lot. Before his wife died, she had always hoped the cottage would be fixed up and someone would love it. When Oscar overheard Grace talking about needing to find a new place to call home, he'd offered to rent her the cottage, fully furnished, if she agreed to slowly work on the place. Paint, refinishing the floors, stuff that required a little elbow grease.

"Take this up with your father." She slid the chain off and opened the door. "Not me."

"Terminate your lease early. You'll get back your deposit. I'll even throw in extra for the inconvenience.

Let's say two months' worth of rent. That's a generous offer."

Indeed, it was. Too bad it came hand in hand with despicable harassment. "No, thanks." She narrowed her eyes at him. "I like living here."

"I've been nice about this so far. But we can do this the hard way."

Pinpricks of fury needled her spine. The one thing she would never tolerate was a bully. "Get out."

"This isn't over. Do you hear me? You think me sitting in your living room gave you a fright?" He gave a dark chuckle filled with pure evil. "Girlie, you haven't seen anything yet."

The threat hit her like a physical touch slithering across her skin, making it hard not to tremble.

"Ooh, I'm scared," she said, her voice cutting like steel, though her nerves were rubbed raw. "Quaking in my boots."

"You should be."

"I think you're forgetting something."

Rodney cocked an eyebrow. "What's that?"

"My brother is the sheriff. He won't take too kindly to you threatening me."

With a cruel, determined smile, Rodney stepped closer, crowding her space. He reeked of cigarettes and beer, making her stomach turn. "Word is he's on vacation. For a couple of weeks. Twelve days to be precise. Visiting his girlfriend all the way in Paris, trying to win her back after she dumped him. Isn't that right?"

A shiver went down her spine. Apparently, *word* had

spread despite Daniel's discretion, and it had been chillingly accurate.

Then she realized Rodney hadn't pulled a stunt of this magnitude before now. He had waited, biding his time until her only family and source of protection was gone. Leaving her vulnerable.

"A lot can happen in two weeks," he sneered. "Be so much easier if you packed up and moved on."

Now Grace was having a different kind of fantasy. About kicking this pig between his legs. Or punching him. In the throat. "Leave. Now."

"Or what?"

She was going to make her fantasy a reality.

Selene had made certain Grace knew how to defend herself so she would never be the victim of date rape or an aggressive bully who wanted to get physical. She was no expert by any stretch of the imagination, but thanks to five years of Krav Maga, she was no pushover, either. Through self-defense classes she had learned to overcome the challenge of her petite build, but she didn't want Rodney to know that. In the event he took her on, he was still a big guy and a punch from him would pack a wallop. If he thought she was helpless, it might work to her advantage one day.

For now, she backed up, keeping her eyes on him, and snatched the shotgun from above the fireplace. It was loaded and Daniel had taught her how to use it.

She pointed it at his chest. "Or you'll regret it."

He glared at her but left, slamming the door behind him.

Next time he lurked in the dark in her cottage, she

wouldn't be able to rely on the shotgun. Rodney might unload it.

Perhaps it was time to buy a handgun to keep in her purse.

She went to the door and quickly turned the bolt and threw on the chain, as though she could lock the devil out.

At the window, she pulled back the curtain to be sure Rodney was leaving. He stormed off to the side of the property into a dense grove of dark, shadowy pine trees. He lived with his father a couple of miles away in that direction, but she doubted he had walked to the cottage. Not at night in the cold.

Headlights flashed on in the cluster of trees, igniting another hot flare of anger in her. The SOB had hidden his truck so she wouldn't have any idea he was lurking inside.

Rodney pulled off in his pickup and turned down the gravel road, but a wave of relief didn't follow. Although he was gone, for now, she suspected that he was right.

His words tumbled through her head. *A lot can happen in two weeks.*

This wasn't over. It was just the beginning.

"Give it your best shot, Rodney." Because she wasn't breaking her lease.

Not without a fight.

Chapter Four

Beyond the gate surrounding the Shining Light compound, the glass and steel of the main building gleamed silver in the morning sunshine. Pulling up to the guardhouse that was the size of a toll booth, Holden was glad that Special Agent Becca Hammond had decided to accompany him. Having an expert on the cult be there during the interview would give him a greater degree of insight.

As an armed guard approached, Holden rolled down the window.

"Morning," the man said. He wore jeans, boots, a dark gray knit pullover beneath a heavyweight jacket. "May the light shine upon you."

Holden cleared his throat at the greeting. "I'm Chief Deputy Holden Powell. This is Special Agent Hammond, and back there is Deputy Russo. We're here to speak with Marshall McCoy."

The guard narrowed his eyes to slits. *"Empyrean,"* he said, "is unavailable unless you have an appointment or a warrant."

Holden smiled. "We have neither. Just want to talk.

About one of your own, back in town. She's dead. We'd appreciate it if your leader," he said, refusing to use the title McCoy had given himself, "could spare us a moment of his time."

"One minute." The guard returned to the gatehouse. Inside, he closed the door and picked up a phone.

Holden couldn't overhear the discussion, but he doubted they would have any problem getting in. Death tended to open doors.

The medical examiner had confirmed the young woman's neck had been broken during a fall off the balcony of the landing. Based on the way her body had landed, she had been pushed. The ME also found marks on her neck consistent with strangulation. Grace had been right about the assailant choking the victim prior to the fall.

While getting a statement from the other guest staying at the B and B, Ashley had learned the silver truck was a rental belonging to Hughes, the out-of-towner. The scratches hadn't been there prior to him going to bed. Which meant they had forensics to tie the motorcycle to the scene of the crime.

Find the bike, find the killer.

The security guard finally hung up the phone. A buzzer sounded. Then the gate rolled open. "Drive up to the main building. Someone will meet you there."

Holden tipped his hat in thanks.

They drove up the long, paved drive slowly. The building sat on a hill, overlooking the rest of the property.

"Those are the barracks." Becca Hammond pointed to four smaller buildings, large cabins really, set off to the side. Farther east was an expansive meadow. On the periphery was what appeared to be a chapel and work buildings. "Everyone lives there except for Empyrean and his family."

Not surprising. The man in charge had the best residence—one that looked down on all the others.

"Are they like dorms?" Ashley asked.

Becca shook her head. "Not like what you're thinking of from college. The setup is closer to that of bunkhouses."

That meant the barracks consisted of a large open room with narrow beds for each individual, communal bathrooms and little privacy. His family's ranch had a bunkhouse for the cowboys working there.

"They're almost completely self-sufficient here," Becca said. "They grow all their own food, make most of their clothing and sell handmade goods for the rest of what they need."

Adjacent to the main house was a detached garage with ten bays. Some of the doors were up, revealing a couple of the white Shining Light vans and several motorcycles.

He wished he had already gotten Grace's statement since she was the only one who had seen precisely what the assailant had been driving. There was a wide variety of motorcycles with differing body styles as well as engines.

The ones visible in the garage were dual-sport motorcycles. Designed to be slim for agility when going off-road. Great for commuting without lugging around much weight.

He had only ever seen their vans around town. It was too bad he hadn't known the Shining Light used motorcycles. Otherwise, he would've brought Grace along to see if any looked familiar.

At least he hoped she was sleeping in and had been able to get a good night's rest. Although the hospital had considered her fit enough to be released, last night she had looked weary and unwell. And nonetheless captivating.

In the car, when she'd tilted her head and looked at him, there it had been, that irritating and wondrous tug of attraction.

And he hated it—that visceral urge. To know her better. To draw closer to her. Touch her.

Kiss her.

He almost had, until sanity stopped him.

She was so pretty and sweet. Fearless, too, which was an irresistible combination to him. He'd been with attractive women before, but none that he'd been drawn to. It was much more than her looks that fueled the internal battle he fought every time he was around her.

A battle he didn't want. Didn't need. Actually, he couldn't afford to lose it, giving in to that primal attraction. Not with Grace Clark.

Unfortunately, she was the only one who made him feel anything good.

"What's the deal with the big building?" Ashley asked.

"They use it for almost everything. Meetings. Education. Counseling. The dining hall. Movie night. Celebrations. Also, Empyrean and his adult children live there. A son and a daughter."

Ashley leaned forward, putting a hand on Becca's seat. "How do you know so much about the inner workings if you've never been inside the compound?"

"I pick up tidbits here and there," Becca said nonchalantly.

A few months ago, Nash had confided in Holden that their task force had gotten a huge boon. Becca had managed to convince someone inside the ranks of the Shining Light to be a confidential informant. That fact was privileged information, usually need-to-know only, and as a liaison with the task force, he'd been brought into the loop. Also, unlike the rest of the town, Nash still trusted him.

Holden would never endanger that person, whoever it was, since he didn't know their identity.

All he could say for certain was that after Becca had taken a look at the deceased, she'd been relieved that it hadn't been her informant.

In front of the wide stone steps of the building, Holden threw the gear in Park. As they got out of the vehicle, another guard greeted them.

"Please follow me." The security guard led the way up the steps.

This one was unarmed, no holster on his hip and no telltale bulge of one under his jacket. But Holden had no doubt men with weapons were watching them. The Shining Light had an arsenal on this compound. Illegal arms that had become the focus of the joint task force, which aimed to find the supplier and shut them down.

They were shown into the sweeping two-story foyer

of the building. The place was immaculate, flooded with light from the floor-to-ceiling windows.

The guard unzipped and removed his jacket and hung it on a coat rack next to the door. He was dressed the same as the other at the gate, wearing a gray knit sweater.

The Shining Light didn't have a caste system, but everyone had a function and wore a color that represented it. Security donned gray. Basic workers, green, like Skye. Artists, musicians—the creatives—wore orange. Yellow was reserved for counselors and educators. New recruits considering whether to join could be singled out by the color blue.

When they came to town as a group, to hawk their goods or to spread the word about their way, they wore Shining Light T-shirts that had the address, a phone number to the compound and an email on the back. En masse, they were something to see.

A smiling troop of calling cards, spouting love and forgiveness.

"Remove your shoes," the security guard said as he took off his steel-toe boots.

"Are you serious?" Holden asked. "Is it really necessary?" Didn't seem very professional to take off his boots like this was a social visit.

"He's quite serious," a man said, appearing at the top of the staircase. "We live here. Eat here. Commune here. Our family puts forth great effort to keep things tidy. All we ask is that you respect their hard work by not tracking in dirt."

Put that way, the request sounded reasonable. Still, Holden bristled, not liking it.

Becca didn't hesitate in taking off her boots. Ashley shrugged and followed suit. Not wanting to make a big deal out of it, Holden did likewise.

The man sauntered down the ridiculously dramatic grand staircase. With bright green eyes and sandy-blond hair that fell below his collar, he looked sophisticated in tailored slacks, a T-shirt, blazer—all in white—and bare feet.

No hand-knit clothing for Marshall McCoy.

"Welcome to the Shining Light," he said, extending his arms wide. His necklace—a pendant of a half-moon and sun—gleamed in the sunshine. "I'm Empyrean."

Holden made the round of introductions. "We'd like to ask you a few questions."

"Of course. I was told you wish to speak with me about an urgent matter. Please come with me."

McCoy led them down a long hall to a set of double doors and showed them into an office that must've also served as a library. Holden had never seen so many bookshelves packed tight in a home office. Then again, nothing about this place was ordinary.

A large mahogany desk faced two chairs. The room was spacious enough to comfortably fit a long sofa as well. The back windows brought in lots of natural light and overlooked a greenhouse and garden that must have been gorgeous in the summer.

They all sat, Holden and Becca taking the chairs. Ashley sat to the side on the sofa. Looking around the room, Holden realized he hadn't seen any curtains or blinds in any of the windows.

"Thank you," McCoy said to the guard. "You may leave us."

"But they're armed, sir."

"We're law enforcement," Holden said, confused as to why this was a necessary discussion. "Here on official business."

His comment didn't erase the concerned expression on the guard's face.

"It's okay." McCoy gave the man a reassuring look. "They mean us no harm. Feel free to leave the doors open if it will put your mind at ease."

"As you wish." The guard touched his necklace, the same as the one McCoy wore, as he bowed his head and eased out of the office, keeping the doors wide-open.

"I understand that one from my flock has passed on," McCoy said, growing somber.

"She was murdered," Holden corrected.

McCoy frowned. "How did it happen?"

"We're not at liberty to say. We were hoping you could identify her for us. She went by the name Skye Starlight."

McCoy leaned back in his chair, tilted his head up and closed his eyes. "My goodness. Skye will be sorely missed. She was a bright star among us."

"What was her real name?" Holden asked.

Opening his eyes, McCoy fixed him with a stare. "Skye Starlight is her real name. Or rather *was*. All who join my flock are reborn. In that sacred ceremony, they shed their former selves and are given the surname

Starlight. Then they choose a new forename. You are a guest. Do not disrespect our ways while here."

"He meant no disrespect," Becca said. "What was Skye's name when she came to you?"

"Emma Burk."

Holden didn't voice the profanity that sprang to his mind. Sure enough, he knew her. Simply hadn't recognized her. *Emma.* Daughter of Lorraine and Gary. The Burks had three children, all spaced three years apart in age. Todd, the eldest, was thirty-two. Kyle was the middle child. That made Emma twenty-six at the time of her death.

Lorraine and Gary lived over on Sudley Drive and owned the Custom Gears Garage, located across the street from their home. The garage was first doing basic automotive repairs, and still did, but over the last fourteen years had begun specializing in motorcycles. They'd been handling all the business for the Iron Warriors—an outlaw motorcycle gang—once Todd became a member.

"Why wasn't she here at the compound?" Becca asked. "What was she doing in town?"

"Skye went to visit her secular family."

Holden took out his notepad and pen. "Did she leave often to visit them?"

"Every month, for three days."

"Why only three?" Holden asked, recalling that Mr. Quenby told him how the deceased *had* to leave.

"Each phase of the moon lasts a little over three days. So no member is allowed to be gone longer than that from the compound."

"Allowed?" Becca asked, wanting to dig deeper into the same word that had piqued Holden's curiosity. "What exactly does that mean?"

"There are rules here, just as there are beyond our gate. To be a member of my flock means you have agreed to abide by them."

"And what happens if someone breaks your rules?" Becca asked.

"There are consequences. I would not be a good shepherd if there weren't."

"Please elaborate on the nature of those consequences." Holden gestured for him to speak when McCoy hesitated.

"It depends on the rule broken. For example, if Skye had stayed away longer than three nights, then she would not have been allowed to spend the night away from the compound the following month. Break that rule three times and you are asked to leave the flock." McCoy set his forearms on the desk and clasped his hands. "Before you ask, we do not engage in corporal punishment. And anyone is free to leave our family permanently at any time. No one is forced to be here. The way of the light is a choice made with a willing heart and an open mind."

Sounded good. Maybe too good to be true. "Was anyone here upset about Skye's trips away from the compound?"

McCoy stiffened. "You're asking if anyone here killed her. The answer is no. She came to us broken, addicted to drugs and suicidal. I saved her, pulling her back from the brink. This family embraced her, got her clean and loved her."

The last time Holden had seen Emma she had been strung out on drugs and looked like hell. Dirty, drawn, her eyes sunk into her head. A stone-cold junkie, making her parents' lives miserable.

Cleaned up and sober, she had been unrecognizable from the woman she had once been.

"Whoever killed Skye," McCoy added, "is out there, beyond our gates, living in the darkness." He rose from his seat. "If that's all?"

Holden stood. "How long was she a member?"

"She was reborn unto us almost a year ago. The celebration of her rebirth was to take place in January."

"If it's so perfect here," Holden said, "why did Skye visit her secular family so often?"

"To see her three-year-old daughter, Amelia."

The child in the photograph. "Do you not allow children here?" Holden asked, putting away his notepad.

"We have many children. All are welcome here regardless of age. Skye lost custody of her daughter to her parents before she joined us. A bond between a mother and child is special. I persuaded her to initiate the visits. Even gave her special dispensation to see Amelia every Sunday for a few hours after worship, but her parents wanted Skye to stick to the three-day window once a month to minimize disruption to the little girl's schedule. That's why I encouraged Skye to seek custody. I even paid Mr. Nagle, a family lawyer, to give her advice on how to proceed."

Becca exchanged a glance with Holden that told him she was thinking the same thing as him.

Marshall McCoy had just given them a motive for

murder. Fighting over custody of a child could get emotionally charged. Easy for things to turn nasty.

Even deadly.

Before picking up Grace, his next stop would be to the Burks'.

Chapter Five

As the rideshare stopped in front of the pastry shop, Divine Treats, Grace rated the driver and confirmed payment. "Thanks," she said, hopping out.

There was no sense in Holden trekking all the way across town to pick her up when she was capable of getting herself there.

Entering the bakery, she was hit full force by the smell of sugary goodness, which sparked her appetite for the first time today. She'd been a bundle of nerves since discovering Rodney in her home. Sleep had been impossible, with her thoughts racing a mile a minute. She could barely rest or eat. The idea of breakfast had made her queasy until right now.

Amy, one of the clerks, waved. "You're in earlier than usual."

"Figured I'd get a jump on things."

"The order for Delgado's is ready." Amy hiked her chin toward the six pies boxed and tied up with string. "I included a little something for you, too."

Every Friday Amy gave her a sweet treat. "Please tell me it's a chocolate croissant."

"I saved you the last bear claw."

Grace salivated. "Even better. You're an angel."

"I know." Amy winked. "Hey, I take classes over at USD," she said, referring to the Underground Self-Defense school Grace had seen nearby. It was owned by a woman, Charlie Sharp. "There's a female-only class I wanted to invite you to."

"Oh, I, um, know how to throw a punch and a kick."

"Figured it might be a good way for you to meet people. Sometimes the ladies get a drink together afterwards. It's Thursday evenings."

"I'm committed to working Thursdays until after the Super Bowl." So Xavier could watch football.

"There won't be any more classes until after the New Year. You could always start in February. Think about it."

"Okay. I will." Grace grabbed the bundle of pies along with the little brown bag sitting on top. She'd never been good at making friends. Something so simple was always so hard for her. Maybe the class would be a good opportunity. "Have a good one."

"Merry Christmas."

"To you, too." It was hard to believe Christmas was around the corner, only three days away.

Grace pushed back through the doors outside. Her gaze flew to the decorations hanging on storefronts and draped from the lampposts. Since everything had been put up before Thanksgiving, she'd grown numb to it. Perhaps pushed the thought of being alone for the holidays to the back of her mind to ward off the sadness.

She loved the quaint streets and the small-town,

homey feel. Even though, technically, it was a city. There were lots of murals on the walls to catch your eye, little pops of fascinating art in places where she would least expect.

Delgado's was right down the street, which made these regular pickups easy to do on foot. The best part about this morning routine was the walk back to the bar and grill. The Snowy Range Mountains were a breathtaking backdrop that she doubted she'd ever tire of, much less take for granted. It wasn't the ocean, but the abundance of natural beauty more than made up for it.

Xavier Triggs was standing out in front of the bar and grill, waiting on her. She'd called him this morning, asking him to come in a little early.

He took the pies from her while she fished her keys from her coat pocket. "I still can't believe what happened to you. I saw the police tape outside the B and B. You could've been killed."

She had been fortunate. Unlike the woman she had tried and failed to help. "Thanks for getting here early." She unlocked the door, and they went inside. "I have a feeling today is going to be hectic."

"Speaking of hectic. I hate to be the bearer of bad news, but I have an item to add to your to-do list."

"What's that?"

"When I parked out back, I noticed you had two flat tires."

"Two?" Grace winced.

She had just put snow tires on her brand-new-to-her *used* Chevy Blazer. She'd bought it after being left no choice but to trade in her cherry-red Mazda MX-5. For the weather and terrain of Wyoming, the sporty convertible, with its sleek lines, had been impractical.

"Unfortunately. Both tires on the same side. Don't you live off Old Mill Road?" Xavier asked. "That rural stretch is all dirt and gravel."

"Yeah." Out in the boonies, where the road didn't get plowed regularly. Hence the need for snow tires.

"When the grader evens out the road, the blade can sharpen the edges of the stones. You must've had the bad luck to roll over some jagged rocks."

To her knowledge, the grader hadn't been through since October. "I wonder how much that's going to cost me."

"Three to six hundred depending on what kind of tires you get."

Ouch. That was an expense she hadn't budgeted for. Thankfully her online classes for her master's degree in healthcare administration had been cheaper than she'd expected. "Great."

"Maybe you can get them patched rather than shelling out for new ones. You should ask."

"I'll call a local garage and have them tow it. Do you have any idea which one is closest?"

"General Tire and Automotive."

She googled them, looked up their number and called, making arrangements. It had been simple and there wouldn't be a four-hour wait like she would've had in Los Angeles. Then again, her tires wouldn't have gotten punctured on gravel out there, either.

"One of the guys is coming over now to get it."

"Hey, if you need to run errands, or want to take

the day off," Xavier said, "I can cover down. After I told my wife about what happened to you, she gave me an earful this morning about letting you close so I can watch football."

He didn't *let* her do anything. She was the one doing the letting. "I make the schedule. What happened isn't your fault."

"Other than giving your statement at the sheriff's office, do you think they'll need you for anything else?"

Good question. "I don't know." Grabbing her phone again, she fired off a text to Holden.

At Delgado's. Saved u a trip. Ready to give my statement. Or help any way I can.

GLANCING AT THE TEXT, Holden, now alone in the car, grumbled to himself. She was so headstrong. He'd never met a woman like Grace. He had nothing against independence or strength. His mother had both. But Grace had a perplexing mix of steel and fragility. He couldn't wrap his head around it. Or rather her. It was as though she had a wall around herself, closing herself off. He couldn't pinpoint why.

Whatever the reason, it compelled her to do everything on her own instead of relying on others. Or waiting for help. That was what had made her go outside in a rainstorm with a baseball bat and had nearly gotten her killed.

She was unpredictable and enjoyed challenging him. Which he loved, unexpectedly. There was something about Grace Clark that made him want to know all her secrets.

Then again, the more he knew, the more he was drawn to her, the more easily her charms would weaken his resolve to do the smart thing and not kiss her.

Holden drove past Custom Gears Garage and parked across the street in front of the Burks' residence, behind a pickup truck. No motorcycles in the driveway, but the garage was closed.

His arrival drew attention. Kyle Burk looked up from a computer in the office that faced the road and stared at him. As soon as Holden strode up the walkway of the house, Kyle was out of his seat and hustling into the garage where they worked on the vehicles.

Standing at the front door, he waited to ring the bell. He only wanted to deliver the bad news once while assessing reactions. Then he would launch into his line of questioning, which he didn't want interrupted.

"Holden," Gary called as he crossed the street. Kyle was right behind his father. "What's going on? Why are you here?"

That was when he rang the bell.

It didn't surprise him in the least that both Gary and Kyle were rushing over to find out what had brought Holden to their doorstep. Not like it was every day a sheriff's deputy came knocking.

By the time Lorraine answered the door, her husband and son had entered the front yard.

"Can we all go inside?" Holden asked. "I need to speak with you."

"Certainly." Stepping aside, Lorraine glanced at her

watch. "I have some time before I need to leave. It's my turn to help out with lunch prep at Amelia's preschool."

Taking off his hat, Holden crossed the threshold. Kyle was the last to file in. When he shut the door, Holden noticed the cast on his right arm. It had a fresh look to it, as though the injury had been recent.

"I think it's best if we sit down," Holden said.

Heading toward the living room, Lorraine sighed. "If this is about Todd getting caught doing something illegal with that club of his, we are *not* bailing him out."

Once the Burks were all seated in a row on the couch, Holden took a chair opposite them. "Todd hasn't been arrested. I'm here about Emma." Swallowing, he paused. "She's dead."

The color slowly drained from Lorraine's face.

Gary shook his head like he was confused. "What?"

"Oh no," Kyle said in a low voice.

"Dead…" Lorraine pressed a palm to her chest. "That can't be. We just saw her yesterday. She was fine."

"This must be a mistake," Gary said.

Kyle wrapped his good arm around his mother's shoulders. "Are you sure it's Emma?"

"I'm very sorry. There is no mistake." Though Holden wished it were. "A witness saw Emma fighting with someone. A man. He was seen choking her shortly before she died. But we haven't been able to identify him because his face was covered."

"Wait a minute." Gary scooted to the edge of the sofa. "Are you saying that she was murdered?"

Holden nodded. "Yes."

"She's really dead?" Lorraine said on a sob, dissolving under the shock of losing her only daughter.

Kyle tightened his embrace on his mother.

"Was it drug-related?" Gary asked. "We always thought she'd get hooked back on heroin or meth."

"It's like you said, Mom. Once a junkie, always a junkie."

Shivering and weeping, Lorraine hung her head and covered her mouth with a hand.

"There's no evidence that she'd been using. We believe she was clean, but won't know for certain until we get the results of the toxicology tests," Holden said, wanting to alleviate their concerns. That didn't mean this wasn't drug-related. Or that it wasn't connected to a custody battle. "I'm sorry for your loss. I know this is difficult, but it's imperative that we find out all we can as quickly as possible to increase the likelihood of us catching the person who did this. Do you mind answering a few questions?" Each gave their consent with a nod. "You mentioned seeing Emma yesterday." Holden took out his pad and pen. "What time did she leave here?"

"I don't know," Lorraine said, her voice breaking.

Gary lifted a shoulder. "We had dinner together at about five thirty. Emma gave Amelia her bath. Read her a few stories." Gary paused, like he was thinking about what to say next. "Then she left." His gaze darted away from him.

Holden didn't know if that was because he was lying or hiding something. But it was one or the other. "So would you say she left around seven, eight, maybe nine o'clock?"

"Closer to nine," Gary said with a nod.

"That's right," Kyle added, sitting upright like he'd remembered something. "The detective show Mom likes had just started but she was too upset to watch it."

Holden's mind snagged on the word *upset*, but decided he'd circle back around to it. Something about that time frame was off. He didn't know much about kids, but he suspected there shouldn't be such a big gap between dinner and when a child went to sleep. "Lorraine, what time does Amelia go to bed?"

"Seven thirty," she said without hesitation. "We like to keep her on a schedule."

Holden looked between them. "Then why did Emma stay for an extra hour and a half?"

Kyle lowered his head.

Clearing his throat, Gary climbed to his feet. "I'll get you some tissues, sweetheart, and a glass of water." He shuffled out of the room.

"Lying to me is obstruction of justice," Holden said.

Lorraine cried harder, sobbing uncontrollably. The sounds she made were closer to whimpers than wails. She opened her mouth, then reconsidering, closed it.

"Why was Emma here until nine?" Holden kept his voice calm, low and firm. "Why were you too upset to watch your show?"

Again, Lorraine took her time, swallowing like there was a lump in her throat. "She wanted to talk to us. About getting custody back and taking Amelia."

Gary returned from the kitchen. His wife accepted the box of tissues but waved off the glass of water.

"Did you fight about it?" Holden asked.

Lorraine nodded. "We had a terrible argument. Said awful things to each other. Oh, God, Gary." She turned to her husband as if suddenly remembering, and the look she sent his way ripped at Holden's heart. "The last thing we said to her was—"

"We didn't mean it," Gary said, cutting her off. His face seemed to break apart. His eyes glistened as tears slid down his cheeks. "The stuff we said had only been out of anger. Because we were caught up in the heat of the moment. Nothing more. Emma knew we loved her."

The heat of the moment often sparked a firestorm of trouble. Crimes of passion, especially homicides, were the result of a sudden strong impulse such as rage rather than as a premeditated act.

"Did anyone give her a lift somewhere?" Holden asked.

"No." Kyle shook his head. "We were just relieved when she left. Mom was worried Dad was going to have a stroke or a heart attack."

"It's my understanding that you let her stay here at the house during previous visits."

"Yes," Gary said. "I'd pick her up near the compound and bring her to the house because it's such a long way to walk. That way she could maximize every minute with Amelia."

It sounded like they supported the visits until this last one. "Did you pick her up a few days ago?"

Gary nodded. "Sure did."

"What were you driving?"

"My Ford," Gary said. "The F-150 parked outside."

"You still ride, don't you?" Holden asked. "What kind of motorcycle do you have?"

"Couple of Harleys. A Low Rider ST and a Fat Boy 114. They're both in the garage. Why?"

"What about you, Kyle?"

"I don't have my own. Sometimes Dad will let me ride one of his."

"Why didn't you let Emma stay at the house this time?" Holden asked, his gaze bouncing between the parents.

Lorraine wiped her nose with a tissue and dabbed at her eyes. "She brought up the custody issue last month. We were worried that if she stayed at the house during this visit, we'd only bicker the entire time. That would not have been good for Amelia."

"I imagine you feel that your granddaughter is better off here than she would have been with Emma."

"You hold on a minute." Gary pointed a finger at him. "We've raised Amelia since she was a baby because Emma was high all the time. Then she joined that weird cult, where they brainwashed her."

That was one interpretation. "Got her clean, from what I've heard," Holden said.

"Yeah, they did." Gary propped a fist on his thigh. "With that Empyrean proselytism. He turned our daughter into some kind of puppet. She wasn't the same person anymore. Who knows what would happen to an impressionable, innocent child in that compound? Yes, we are what's best for Amelia. But we never wanted anything to happen to Emma. Never." The man had a shell-shocked expression that seemed genuine. "She was our daughter. Until you have a kid you can't understand that kind of unconditional love."

Holden mulled that over a moment. "Where were the three of you between eleven and midnight last night?"

"Right here," Gary said, stabbing a finger toward the floor. "In bed. Asleep. Lorraine had a terrible migraine. I set the alarm once Emma left. A habit after she started using."

"I wasn't asleep." Kyle looked at Holden as he rubbed his mother's back. "I was in bed, watching TV. Bingeing a show."

Kyle was a grown man living at home with his family. Not that Holden could criticize him for it. He was thirty years old himself and still living on his parents' ranch. Though it was in an apartment above the garage, where he could come and go with some relative privacy. Not in the basement, like Kyle. But the difference was purely semantics.

"Did Emma say where she was going?" There were several hours unaccounted for between the time she left the Burks' and when Grace had called about the fight.

"To see her ex, Jared Simpson," Kyle said. "Amelia's father."

"That man is bad news." Gary swore under his breath. "Jared is the one who got Emma hooked on drugs in the first place. He used her as a drug mule and even had her selling for him. She started seeing him again. Last month. I don't know what she was thinking."

"They had an unhealthy and volatile relationship," Kyle said.

"Volatile in what way?" Holden asked.

"They had physical altercations," Lorraine said. "There are medical records at the hospital documenting it. She almost lost Amelia while pregnant."

Holden nodded. He would have Mitch look into it and dig up the records. Becca was already doing him a favor by tracking down the lawyer Nagle, to see what they could glean from him. "I'll get out of your way. I'm sorry for your loss." Holden put on his hat. "Kyle, see me to the door."

Gary held his wife and rocked, taking over comforting her while Kyle walked with him.

At the front door, Holden whispered, "What did your parents say to Emma that was so awful? I need to know."

Kyle glanced at his grieving parents before stepping outside on the front stoop with him and closed the door. "Emma OD'd a couple of times. The last incident happened right before she joined the Shining Light. Mom called her selfish, ungrateful, brainwashed by McCoy." Kyle took a deep breath. "Dad was furious. He said that it would have been better if they hadn't saved her life after she overdosed. The whole thing was pretty intense."

Holden could only imagine. "Did you back your parents up in the argument? Or take Emma's side?"

Kyle shook his head. "I stayed out of it. Mostly listened. Tried to keep my dad from getting too upset."

"That's understandable," Holden said. "What happened there?" He gestured to Kyle's cast.

"Accident in the repair shop. I broke my hand. Really stupid on my part."

Holden wondered if it had been an accident.

The Burks had a history of violence. At least two of their children did anyway. Todd used to beat up kids in school. These days he was beating up his girlfriend, or as the bikers would call her, his old lady. Each time he did it, Nikki never agreed to file charges against him. Still, the courts had him taking mandatory domestic violence classes.

There was also Emma. Allegedly, she'd gotten into physical fights with Jared on multiple occasions.

Oftentimes children who had survived domestic violence were at risk for future abusive relationships. Perhaps the cycle of violence had started with Gary. Maybe it was still ongoing. This time with Kyle's hand.

"When did it happen?" Holden asked, staring at the cast.

"Last week."

With a broken hand, Kyle wasn't choking anyone or riding a motorcycle. But Gary was about the same build as his son. An inch or two shorter, with a bit of a belly that came with age and a few beers. He also owned two motorcycles and had been angry and wishing his daughter hadn't survived.

"Since we're out here," Holden said, "do you mind opening the garage and showing me the motorcycles?"

"Sure, come on."

Kyle opened the garage and turned on the overhead light.

The Low Rider was gauntlet gray, with a wide base

and saddlebags. Designed for a weekend escape out on the open road. The Fat Boy was sleek. Fast. Perfect for a hot rod rider.

And it was black.

Holden inspected the left side of the bike, where it would've been damaged. No spots stuck out as being recently buffed and repainted. Both bikes gleamed like they were well-maintained and not used often.

There were a lot of motorcycles in town. Most of them were black.

But how many had owners who knew Emma well enough to kill her?

Off the top of his head, Holden could think of at least two more.

Jared Simpson and Todd Burk.

"My parents didn't mean what they said to Emma. They were upset and angry, but they didn't want her to die. Last night, Mom told her to be careful going to visit Jared. She always worried that if the drugs didn't kill Emma, then one day Jared would."

Maybe he had.

Chapter Six

Grace sat in the passenger's seat of the sheriff's SUV, looking at a diagram of different motorcycle body types. She'd already eliminated a couple but couldn't be sure which kind it was. "I don't know. That's all I remember."

"Okay, thanks." Holden turned off the recorder he'd placed on the dash, so he could save time by taking her statement while they drove rather than doing it at the station.

"I wish I could be more useful." She wasn't able to identify the man, or the motorcycle he'd been riding. All she could say with certainty was that his helmet had covered most of his face and he'd been wearing gloves.

The motorcycle didn't have a wide frame, which ruled out those with saddlebags. But she couldn't tell if it was some kind of sport bike or cruiser. The diagram only showed a side profile of the motorcycles. It had come at her head-on, but she hadn't even thought to get the license plate number.

"You have more information than you realize," Holden said, driving to the far east side of town, where she hadn't ventured before. "I think if you saw the same motorcycle again, it would help."

Not only seeing it but hearing it. She'd never forget the sound of that engine as it had roared toward her. "You might be right."

"Are you sure you can spare the time to ride along with me?" he asked.

She had already opened Delgado's and Xavier had no problem handling things while she was out. He felt so bad about not being there last night when she got hurt that it seemed as if he'd agree to almost anything.

"I'm positive," she said. "It's the least I could do to help you catch whoever killed Emma." It was strange saying her name. Somehow it only reinforced the connection she felt to the dead woman, strengthening her conviction to seek justice.

Holden pulled up in front of a run-down mobile trailer and swore.

"What's wrong?" Grace asked.

"This is Jared Simpson's place. His motorcycle isn't here, which most likely means that he isn't. I wanted you to take a look at his bike. Give me a sec."

Holden got out and strode up to the front of the mobile home. He banged his fist on the door a couple of times, then waited. There was no answer. He peeked through one of the windows before coming back to the car.

Sitting behind the wheel, he looked around as if thinking about something.

"A penny for your thoughts," she said.

"Jared lives way out here in the middle of nowhere.

Probably so he can cook meth in that trailer. But it's a good four miles from the Burks' house. It would've taken Emma about an hour and a half to get here. So she would've arrived around ten thirty. Let's say she only stayed for ten minutes, that's ten forty. The hike to the B and B would've taken even longer." It was clear on the opposite side of town. "I'd estimate two hours on foot."

"But that would have her arriving at the B and B at half past midnight. Which is too late. She was already dead by then."

"Exactly. That means if she did trek out here, she didn't walk back to the B and B. She was given a ride."

"By the guy on the motorcycle."

Holden nodded.

"Jared?"

"Possibly. Do you know what else isn't too far from Simpson's place?"

She had no idea what he was thinking. "No, what?"

"The Iron Warriors. The motorcycle club has a clubhouse close by. A three-minute drive. And Emma's brother Todd is a member." Holden started the SUV and took off. Using the Bluetooth in the car, he placed a call. "Hey, Ashley, I need you to do something for me."

"Sure, what is it?"

"Track down Jared Simpson. I want him brought in for questioning as a suspect for the Burk case. I was just at his place over on Black Elk Trail. It was empty. Worst-case scenario, I'll need you to sit out front of his trailer until he returns."

Ashley sighed. "All right. One way or another, I'll get him in here. When I do, I'll let you know."

"Thanks." He disconnected the call. "When we get to the club, all of their bikes will be parked outside. Lined up in a nice, neat row. While I'm inside questioning Todd, I want you to look at them. See if any strike you as familiar. But stay in the vehicle."

"Okay. I can do that." Sounded easy enough.

"Don't expect me to be inside too long. Todd has a history of clamming up and then lawyering up. No one has ever been able to convict him on anything. Which is saying a lot considering he's been in trouble since we were in high school."

"You two went to school together?"

"Yeah. Same grade. But we ran in very different social circles. I always thought of him as a bully."

Holden took a left off the road and drove up to a long, single-story building almost half the length of a city block. It must've been the backside, because there weren't any motorcycles.

"That's a clubhouse?" she asked. "Why is it so big?"

"Every member has his own bedroom. When they party and get drunk, they each have a private place to crash. Inside, they've got a bar, game room, armory, conference room, gym, dance area complete with stripper poles. Only goodness knows what else."

"How do you know so much about them?"

"I've got someone who gives me information from time to time. Unfortunately, it's never been anything that would help charges stick."

"What kind of club dues pay for this?"

"It used to be a quarter of the size. Then some of the members, like Todd, got the Iron Warriors involved in drug dealing. Probably other stuff, too. But we've never been able to prove anything."

Holden followed the path along the side of the building and turned in front of the clubhouse. "Hell," he said under his breath. "My timing leaves much to be desired."

A gaggle of men and some women were standing outside, forming a circle around two men having a fistfight. There must've been at least thirty people out there.

Pulling closer slowly, like it was too late to turn back, Holden swore again. "I didn't want them to see you and now it's unavoidable. I was planning to park where the security cameras wouldn't be able to see you. I'm sorry. I don't want any of them giving you a hard time in town."

She caught a glimpse of the back of their black vests and jackets. A silver gauntlet forming a fist, surrounded by a ring of fire.

One by one, heads spun in their direction until everyone's focus was on them, bringing the fight to a stop.

Holden parked a good one hundred feet from the crowd. But they all converged on the car, blocking her view of their motorcycles. "Stay here."

He got out. One man approached Holden, but all the others were close behind.

Grace cracked her window for a little fresh air and to hear the conversation.

"Hey, Rip. I need to speak with Todd."

The man Holden had addressed glanced over his shoulder.

Another guy stepped forward. "What do you want, Holden?" Todd asked, his eyes narrowing as he crossed his arms. A woman came up alongside him, putting a hand on his shoulder.

"Emma's dead," Holden said. "Someone killed her."

Todd didn't react. Didn't flinch. Didn't blink. Nothing from him. "So?" he asked, shrugging a shoulder.

"So, you don't seem too broken up or surprised to hear that your sister is dead."

"Neither is a crime and I'm not bothered because she means nothing to me. The second she became a Starlight, she stopped being my sister. The only family I care about are my brothers here and the blood I've got that goes by Burk. Now, them, I'd do anything for my family, including shed a tear."

Glancing at the clubhouse, Holden said, "Let's get the interview done. It can be here or at the station."

"I'll let you ask three questions, right here," Todd said, pointing at the ground in front of him, "before I decide I no longer feel like cooperating."

Holden drew in a deep breath. "Three isn't very many."

"You're lucky I'm talking at all. I know my rights. I don't have to answer any, but I'm in a charitable mood."

"When was the last time you saw Emma?" Holden asked.

"I haven't seen her since she turned into a Shining Light bootlicker."

Holden folded his arms. "Where were you last night, between eleven and midnight?"

"Here. In bed. Doing things to my old lady—" Todd

nodded to the woman at his side "—that would make you blush."

Pinching her lips, the woman looked away at the car. At Grace. The expression on her face was hard and unyielding, but there was an air of sadness to her.

"Is that true, Nikki?" Holden asked.

"You heard the man," she said.

"Yeah!" a guy in the crowd said. "Todd was here. We all saw him. He didn't leave."

A handful of others spoke up, echoing the same.

"That's three," Todd said. "If you have any further questions, you'll have to ask them with my lawyer present."

"You can try to hide behind your lawyer all you want, but if you killed Emma, no attorney on earth is going to save you. Give Mr. Friedman a heads-up that his services will soon be required."

Todd smirked. "You've got a lot of nerve rolling up in here, wearing that uniform, carrying that badge, like some hero. We all know the truth. You're nothing more than a fraud. Both the old sheriff and your fiancée were neck-deep in a sex trafficking ring right under your nose and you were none the wiser? Come on, man. You're not squeaky-clean. You're as dirty as they come. The real criminal here is you," Todd said, and Grace's gut clenched.

The gang of men standing behind Todd started clapping and whooping and hollering in support. Except for Rip, who stayed stoic and quiet.

"It's about time he was put in his place," someone called out.

"That's what I'm here for, boys, to hold up a mirror in front of this hypocrite's face," Todd said, drawing many cheers and a lot of laughter. "Get out of here." Todd shooed at Holden with his hand. "Charlatan chief deputy."

The knot in Grace's stomach tightened and twisted. Her whole body tensed. Poor Holden must have been mortified, shocked. Wounded.

Holden backed up, slid into the car and threw the gear in Reverse. Once they had enough room, he pulled a U-ey and sped away from the clubhouse.

Awkward silence settled between them.

Holden tightened his grip on the steering wheel. The blood drained from his knuckles until they grew white, his face reddening by the second.

She couldn't stand the quiet any longer. "Holden—"

"Don't." A muscle twitched in his jaw. "Please, don't try to make me feel better because you can't."

"But I—"

He jerked the steering wheel to the right, veering off the road onto the shoulder. Bringing the car to an abrupt stop, he threw open his door and jumped out. He paced in front of the car with his hands on his hips.

Grace gave him a moment to calm down. Then she got out, too. "You can't let him get to you. He's just a bully, like you said." With a posse cheering him on, emboldening him.

Holden kept marching back and forth. For a minute, she wasn't sure if he'd heard her through the haze of anger.

"If it was only Todd and the Iron Warriors, then I

could let it roll off my back. But he only voiced what everyone in this town thinks every time that they look at me. You have no idea what it's like to have everyone doubting you. Wagging their tongues behind your back. Thinking the worst. Looking at you with condemnation even though you did nothing wrong besides trust people who you thought cared about you." He stopped and stared at her. The naked emotion in his unguarded eyes made her heart squeeze. "Damn Jim and Renee. You know she proposed to me, not the other way around. Did I ever tell you that?"

Grace shook her head. He'd never talked about his ex, Renee, or Jim, the previous sheriff. Not until now.

"She did it because Jim told her to. That's how the relationship started. Under Jim's coercion, ordering her to sidle up to me. From the very beginning it was a lie." His voice hollowed. "Like the idiot I am, I said yes because she popped the question in a really public way, putting me on the spot. Not because I loved her, which I realized later that I didn't. And I stayed engaged because it was easy. She never complained. We never argued. She only wanted to make me happy and was so easily satisfied herself. Or so I thought. After she was arrested, she told me she never even liked me as a person. The whole thing had been an assignment for her, a job, to make sure I stayed ignorant to what was really going on. So Jim didn't have to kill me. They both lied and manipulated me. Made me a laughingstock. Robbed me of my dignity. But I guess I should at least be grateful they did it to keep me alive even if it showed everyone what a fool I really am."

Grace stepped toward him, not stopping until she had to tilt her head back to look him in the eyes. "They didn't do that to you as a favor. Jim probably didn't want a murder drawing attention to what he was doing." She put her palm on his chest. "No one can rob you of your dignity. It's an inalienable right. And you're not an idiot or a fool. You simply trusted the wrong people." Grace had been there and done that herself. Her ex, Kevin, had turned out to be thirteen shades of wrong. A gambler with a lousy habit of losing. "You could've quit. Turned in your badge and gone to work on your family's ranch full-time. But you didn't run because you're no coward. Every day you go to work with your head held high, despite the ugly gossip, regardless of the nasty rumors, and you get the job done." Only a man of bone-deep fortitude and determination could do that. "Do you want to know what I see when I look at you?"

The anger dissipated from his face as he calmed, but the pain was still visible. "What?"

She moved her hand from his chest and caressed his cheek, wanting to erase the hurt from his eyes. "A good man with a deeply ingrained sense of honor. Someone trustworthy, funny, smart." Not to mention hot. *"And kind."*

Holden clutched her arms, leaned in and kissed her—a warm press of his lips against hers, lasting just a beat too long to be only friendly.

It was over before she could figure out what to do with her mouth or her hands or if this would ruin things between them.

"Thank you, Grace," he said, his eyes warm, his

voice soft as cotton. "You're a good friend. The sweetest I could ask for."

Her head spun. Her lips tingled. Confusion pulsed through her.

Did he like her? Romantically?

But that wasn't what he had said. She had such limited experience with men, she wasn't sure. Especially based on the way he was looking at her.

Really good friends could kiss on the lips she supposed. It had just been a peck, no tongue, but enough to send heat sliding through her.

The real question was, did she want that kiss to mean more?

Friends were hard to come by. She didn't want to risk losing this one.

Clearing her throat, she averted her gaze. "You're a good friend, too."

They climbed back into the car. Just as Holden started the engine, his cell phone rang. He answered via Bluetooth, putting it on speaker while he drove. "Chief Deputy Powell."

"Hi, Holden, it's Becca. My CI got word to me that Emma seemed happy at the Shining Light. She always followed the rules and was liked by everyone in the compound. No one had any grievances with her or cause to do her harm."

"Okay. That's good to know. Did you track down the family lawyer?"

"Sure did. His office gave me the runaround for a while, but they failed to realize how persistent I can be. Turns out Nagle told Emma that she had a strong case for getting custody of her daughter back because she was sober for almost a year and living in a stable, nurturing environment."

"Why do I sense a *but* coming?" Holden asked.

"*But* he advised her to do anything she could to get the support of the child's father."

"Jared Simpson," he said, glancing at Grace, and she could still feel his lips on hers.

"That's right. If the father supported her claim in court, it would only strengthen her case against the child's grandparents."

"Guess who was allegedly the last person to see Emma alive, according to her parents?"

"Jared."

"Bingo. We're trying to track him down now."

"Want me to see what I can do to help?"

"Any assistance would be much appreciated. The sooner I can question Jared, the better. Thanks." He hung up and looked at her. "Once I have him in the station, can you swing by and take a look at his bike? See if it looks familiar."

"Just let me know. I'll come right over."

Chapter Seven

The day turned out to be more hectic than she had expected. Delgado's had been slammed from one to almost four. The influx of delivery orders had hit them the hardest. They'd all been in walking distance, and she didn't mind doing it. With the nonstop pace, she hadn't gotten a chance to pick up her car after the tire place had called.

Things had finally slowed down, but the dinner rush would begin in a couple of hours.

"Xavier, do you mind covering things for a bit?"

He gave her a weary look. "Sure. Whatever you need. Where are you off to this time?"

"I need to pick up my car, and there's one errand I've been thinking about." What Holden had said about her having more information than she realized kept bugging her. She hated sitting around waiting for him to call to have her look at one bike at a time. There had to be a more efficient way to narrow it down. "Is there a motorcycle showroom around here or a shop that might have a variety of bikes?"

"Are you thinking about buying a motorcycle?"

"No, nothing like that. Do you know a place?"

"There's Custom Gears over on Sudley. They're always working on a bunch of different bikes at the garage. It's owned by the Burk family."

"Any relation to Emma Burk?"

"One and the same. Her dad and brother Kyle work there."

That might be the perfect place. Emma's family must want to help find her killer.

She ordered another rideshare to take her to the tire place. When it arrived, she grabbed her coat and purse. "I'll be back," she said to Xavier, heading for the door.

"Please, hurry."

"I'll do my best."

STANDING IN THE automotive shop, Grace was having a hard time understanding what the mechanic, Ty, was telling her. "What do you mean my car isn't fixed? Why did you call if it wasn't ready? I already authorized you to charge my credit card for new tires if you couldn't patch the old ones."

Ty might have appeared exasperated, but it wasn't reflected in his tone. "Definitely couldn't be patched. But I take it you didn't listen to the message I left?"

No, she hadn't. She had assumed the reason for the call had been to tell her the vehicle was ready. "Did my credit card not go through?" She would've sworn she had a thousand dollars left on it that she had promised herself to only use in case of an emergency. Tires fit the bill.

Ty chewed on a toothpick. "I didn't run the card because I needed to make sure you wanted me to put the new tires on first."

Confusion returned. Amplified. "Were they more expensive than you estimated?"

"Nope. Cheaper actually. Because I gave you a ten percent first-time customer discount."

"Thanks for that." But now, she was the one so exasperated that she had to resist the urge to beat her head against the auto shop wall. "Ty, I haven't had much sleep, it's been a long day, and I have to go back to work and stay there until almost midnight. So if you could please help me understand why you didn't put on the new ones I would appreciate it."

"Easier to show you." He led her to her tires, which had been removed, and pointed at them.

"I can see that they're still flat. Is there something else I'm supposed to be looking at?"

"Both tires have gashes in them." He folded his arms. "Long slices about three inches."

"Okay." She shrugged. "I live on Old Mill, the road with all the gravel. Could a sharp stone have done it?"

"It's possible." Ty looked doubtful. "If that stone was holding a knife."

As she took the time to examine the slashes that had killed her tires, a chill ran through her.

"Have you annoyed or angered anyone recently?" Ty asked. "Someone who might be looking for payback?"

Rodney.

The thought of that man had her blood turning from ice-cold to boiling.

"I can think of one," she said.

"Figured you might want to resolve that issue before I go putting on new tires that might just get slashed again. That would be like lighting three hundred bucks on fire." Frowning, he sighed. "You're a nice lady. Cute, too. I would hate to see you burn money."

She most certainly did not have money to burn. But she also needed a car. "Go ahead and put the tires on."

His frown deepened like it was a decision she might regret. "Are you sure? You might want to go make amends with whoever did this first."

"I am the injured party here." She pointed to her chest. "Not that pig…" Biting her tongue, she swallowed the foul words rising in her throat instead of voicing them. "I've got to have a vehicle. I can't keep paying for a rideshare."

"All right. Suit yourself. Let's burn some money."

She ignored Ty's comment. "How long will it take?"

"An hour. Maybe a little longer."

Looking at the clock on her phone, she rubbed her forehead with the heel of her hand. "I can't afford to waste an hour here. I still have another errand to run before I go back to work. And I really can't afford to take another rideshare."

"Can you drive a stick?" he asked.

Only if she had to. "Yes, why?"

Ty dug in his pocket and pulled out a set of car keys. "You can take my ride to run your errand. Save you a few bucks."

This was a perfect example of what she loved about the Cowboy State. The mechanic at a chain store tire shop in LA never would've made such a kind offer. "Thank you, Ty. I appreciate it."

GRACE JUMPED IN the vintage muscle car and headed for Sudley Drive. Handling the gearshift was like riding a bike. You never forgot. She was familiar with Sudley but had never noticed a repair shop. Then again, she hadn't been looking for one.

It was easy to spot. Hanging over the garage was a huge white sign that had a fist clutching a wrench. She parked, and as she stepped inside the front office, a bell chimed.

A young man with a cast on his arm came up to the reception desk. He had light brown hair that was a little long in the front. His brown eyes were glassy and sorrowful. He was the spitting image of Todd, only younger. His name tag read Kyle. "Afternoon. How can I help you?"

"Are you Kyle Burk?"

"I am."

"My name is Grace Clark. I witnessed what happened to your sister last night. I'm so sorry for your loss."

"Thank you." His brows drew together. "I'm not sure I understand why you're here."

"I want to help your family catch her killer, but I might need your help to do it."

"What can I do?"

"Let me look at some motorcycles. Listen to the engines. Specifically sport bikes and cruisers."

"Not sure how that'll help, but okay." He took her into the open bay of the garage.

The two men who were working on vehicles stopped what they were doing and stared at her.

Kyle ignored them and showed her a red motorcycle. He rattled off a ton of details about it, but the only thing that stuck was that it was a dual sport.

"Could you crank the engine for me?" she asked. "Rev it a bit?"

"Sure." Kyle called over one of the guys gawking, had him climb on and fire it up.

"Can you sit on it the way you would if you were riding on the road?"

From the front, looking at the way he had to lean forward, she didn't think the body style of this vehicle was quite right.

He turned the handgrips, revving the engine for her. The sound was sharp and zippy. Definitely not what she had heard the other night.

"Do all sport bikes sound like this? So high-pitched?"

"More or less," Kyle said. "It has to do with the RPMs, rotations per min at which the different motors operate. Sport bikes operate at a very high RPM range."

That helped. At least she could eliminate another type of motorcycle. "What are the most common cruisers around here?" she asked.

"Harleys, by far," Kyle said, and the other guy nodded in agreement. "We're working on a couple. The good thing about them is they all use big twin engines. Much lower RPM that produces a deeper, heavier sound."

Seemed like a bad thing since it would make it harder to narrow down which kind of cruiser.

They pointed out the Harleys in the shop. As soon as the intense grumble from the engine of one vibrated through her she knew that was the same growl. It was either a Harley or a bike that sounded like it.

Kyle was patient, explaining the differences between the frames, angle of the seats, where a rider would rest his feet, body positioning and so forth. The guy on the bike even pulled up the manufacturer's website on his phone and showed her pictures of the ones they didn't have in the shop.

With their expert guidance, she was able to eliminate any that had windshields or fairings—strategically placed panels that help manipulate airflow. Then based on the positioning of the rider's body on the bike, they narrowed the field further down to a Fat Boy and a Fat Bob. They were very similar. Any differences were slight and none she would be able to discern at night.

"Are you sure it's one of those?" Kyle asked her.

"Not a hundred percent. I mean it was dark and raining. But the driver was right up on me. I'm pretty certain about the body positioning."

"Then it's got to be one of those," the other guy said.

"Does your brother ride a Fat Boy or Fat Bob?" she asked.

Kyle stiffened. "Todd?"

"Yeah," she said.

"I can't help any more." The guy got off the motorcycle. "I've got to get back to work," he said, hurrying away.

The other man in the shop, who'd been eavesdropping the entire time, took out his cell phone and made a call while staring at her.

"Come with me." Kyle hustled outside of the repair shop.

Grace was right on his heels. "What just happened?"

"You can't ask about the MC," he said in a harsh whisper.

"The MC?"

"The motorcycle club. The Iron Warriors. You can't ask about them."

"Why not?"

"Casey is on the phone right now reporting back to them about you," Kyle said, and she glanced over her shoulder at the guy giving someone on the other end an earful. "Go, before one of them shows up. Or worse, Todd does. My brother will cause trouble for you." He turned to go back inside.

"Wait." She put a hand on his forearm, stopping him. "You didn't answer my question. Does Todd ride one of those two motorcycles?"

Kyle swore with a defeated look on his face. "Yes. A Fat Bob. But you didn't hear that from me. Please, leave." His tone was pleading and urgent. "You do *not* want to be on the radar of the Iron Warriors."

Flicking another glance at the guy broadcasting the details of her visit, she feared that was already too late.

Chapter Eight

By the time they had tracked down Jared Simpson at the local strip club, it was eleven thirty at night.

Holden was running on fumes as he sat across the table from Jared in the interrogation room. He'd already been Mirandized before he was persuaded to come in. According to Ashley, Jared had followed her to the station without a single complaint.

"Do you want a lawyer present?" Holden asked.

Narrowing his eyes, Jared asked, "What is this about?"

"The murder of Emma Burk."

Jared swore, his eyes widening in what appeared to be genuine shock. "It wasn't me. I'm innocent. I don't need a lawyer for this."

It wasn't only the guilty who asked for a lawyer. The innocent did, too. But if Jared didn't have one, then it would make this process easier. "When did you last see her?"

"Yesterday evening."

"What time?"

"It wasn't too late." Jared scratched at his unkempt beard. "Maybe ten. Ten thirty."

"Why did she come see you?"

Sighing, Jared rolled his eyes. "She's been trying to get me to support her in a custody case to get Amelia back. Emma wanted to drag our girl to the Shining Light. Wanted me to join them, too," he scoffed. "No way was that ever happening. Emma was a little off her rocker if you ask me. Gary and Lorraine are good people. Solid. Much better parents than either of us."

"How long did she stay at your place?"

"She was only there a hot minute. My girlfriend, Ruby, was not happy to see her. She gets jealous, since Emma and I have a kid together."

"Ruby was there the entire time?"

"Yep."

"Her last name?"

"Belle. Ruby Belle."

"I need to know where to find her." Holden passed him a notepad and pen. "Put down her contact information."

"She was with me at the club," Jared said as he scribbled the information on the paper. "Ruby's a stripper."

"And she wasn't working Thursday night?" Thursday through Saturday were the busiest nights.

"The Iron Warriors shut down the club, hiring most of the strippers for a private party at their clubhouse."

"Why didn't Ruby go? I've heard they're good tippers."

"Yeah," Jared said on a chuckle, "because they want the girls to do more than strip. Only the single gals go to a party like that. Ruby was holed up with me Thursday."

"Did you and Emma fight while she was there?"

"She tried to rope me in to her mess, and I told her flat out that I wasn't getting involved. I wasn't going to open the door to the Shining Light suing me for child support if she won. Her parents don't hassle me for any money," he said, sounding like the deadbeat dad that he was. "Then she threatened me."

"Physically?"

Jared shook his head. "No. She told me that the one-year anniversary of her rebirth over at the cult was coming up. In the days leading up to it, she's supposed to share all the dirt on her former life. The way I hear it, Empyrean uses it to blackmail people who aren't members. Plenty of shady people in her past for her to spill her guts about, but I warned her not to say anything about me. Or the Iron Warriors."

"Warned her how? By threatening to kill her?"

"No, sirree." Jared shook his head emphatically. "I simply told her that I was going to let Todd know."

Everything circled back to him. "What dirt did she have on him and the MC?"

Jared's mouth set in a hard line. "Let's just say she knew about all the felonious activity going on."

"Care to elaborate?"

"I do not. And if you push this, then I'll need a lawyer before I say anything else."

Because he would run the risk of incriminating himself. It must be drug-related. Jared already had a criminal record for dealing. His former relationship with Emma revolved around heroin and meth.

"How did Emma get caught up in the dealings of the Iron Warriors?"

"Todd."

The guy with an alibi. Though Holden wondered how solid it was. Sure, his Iron Warrior brothers would bleed and die and lie for each other, but maybe Nikki was the weak link to test.

"Did you give Emma a ride anywhere that night?"

"I would've offered her one because it was cold and supposed to rain, but I didn't want to upset Ruby. So I didn't. I told Emma to try to get back to the B and B before the storm hit. Maybe call someone for a ride. Or she'd catch pneumonia in that thin jacket she had on."

"Did she use your phone to call anyone?"

"Nah. No way Ruby would've been okay that. My girl wanted Emma to figure it out for herself, without my help."

"What about Todd? Did you call him that night and tell him?" Holden asked. "Don't bother lying. I can always get phone records."

Jared lowered his head and chewed on the inside of his lip. "I gave him a heads-up."

"His response?"

"He didn't sound worried. Said he'd take care of it, like it was no big deal."

"Take care of it how?"

Jared shrugged. "I was smart enough not to ask."

Something he still hadn't been able to account for came back to Holden. "When Emma came to see you that night, was she wearing her Shining Light necklace?"

"Yeah, always."

"Are you sure?"

"She took to fiddling with it whenever she got anxious. I remember her playing with it after I told her I wouldn't help her take the kid away from her parents."

The door opened. Ashley stuck her head in and gave a curt nod, signaling him that Grace was at the station looking at Jared's motorcycle.

"So, am I free to go?" Jared asked.

Not until Ruby had corroborated his version of events. He didn't want to give those two a chance to get their stories straight. "Not just yet. Do we have your permission to collect forensics from your motorcycle? It'll eliminate you as a suspect and once we're done you can leave with your bike."

There were a couple of scratches and dings on his bike. Nothing that looked like damage from an accident, but since they had the bike here, they might as well.

Jared nodded. "Sure."

With that easy consent, the guy was probably telling truth and wasn't the perpetrator. "One more question for you. When you and Emma were together, did she ever say anything about having an abusive childhood?"

"I don't know. I guess she got spankings growing up, but I couldn't tell you if it crossed the line to abuse. She always talked about her parents like they walked on water. Until the Shining Light. She made it sound like her parents might be hard to beat."

Good to know.

The medical records they'd requested on Emma would go back as far as they were available. He would be able to see if those spankings had been something more and whether she had been treated for frequent accidents as a child.

Holden stepped into the hall, closing the door behind him.

"Do you want me or Livingston to go question Ruby?" Ashley asked as they walked.

Livingston had been a deputy longer, but Ashley had been on this case with him from the beginning and had been in the observation room listening to the interview. There was also the fact that she would not allow herself to be distracted by the performances of the girls while at the strip club. Holden wasn't so sure he could say the same about Livingston.

"If you don't mind," Holden said, "I'd like you to go."

Ashley made a gesture of excitement as she whispered, "Yes."

They both grabbed their jackets and hats and headed out of the building. At the sidewalk, Ashley took off for her vehicle.

Holden strode over to Grace, who was waiting patiently. He hoped she hadn't been out in the cold too long. The winter weather seemed to be tough for her to handle, after being in sunny and snowless LA. "Thanks for coming over."

"Timing was perfect," she said with a shiver, rubbing her arms. "I already locked up and after this I'll head home."

He hated her working the late shift, locking up at night alone. But Grace didn't take well to being told what to do. That much he'd learned about her. "Might be best to let Xavier close."

"He does. Sometimes. And whenever I need a little leeway in my schedule because of classes, he's always flexible. We're both team players." Her voice rang with pride.

"What do you think?" He gestured to Jared's motorcycle, which they'd gotten towed to the department. "Could this be it?"

"Definitely not. This bike has a batwing fairing and five-inch windshield," she said, sounding like an expert. "The one from last night didn't have any of this."

It was hard to doubt her certainty. Still, since he'd gotten consent from Jared, he'd run the forensics anyhow, but wouldn't put a rush on it.

"I'm impressed," he said. "Earlier you didn't know zilch about motorcycles. You couldn't tell a fairing from the fuel tank. Care to explain how you've become such an expert in such a short period of time?"

"I did some research." More pride. This time gleaming in her honey-brown eyes.

Holden did his best to restrain the smile tugging at the corners of his mouth. She was so cute, it took some effort, but he suspected that the admiration welling in his chest for her was about to flip to irritation.

"Go on," he said, knowing in his gut there was more to this story. Based on her reluctance to readily share the details, he wasn't going to like what she was about to tell him.

"I went to Custom Gears."

Those five words hit him like a sucker punch. "What?"

"Kyle and this other guy taught me so much. And

before he kicked me out, Kyle admitted that Todd's motorcycle could be the type we're looking for."

"Back up." He drew in a sharp breath. "Why did he kick you out?"

She frowned. "For my protection. Casey, the other mechanic there, called the Iron Warriors and most likely relayed that I had mentioned Todd's name in connection to my thorough research."

"Grace," he said on a huff. "I'm trying to keep you out of the line of fire." Although he hadn't succeeded when he took her to the clubhouse. That had gone terribly. The *entire* MC had seen her, and now Casey had reported that she'd been asking about Todd. "I don't need you rushing headlong into it."

One more thing to add to his list of growing concerns. Grace didn't need trouble with the MC. Neither did the sheriff's department.

But the hornet's nest had been stirred. And there would be repercussions.

Straightening, she hiked her chin up like she was getting ready to argue with him. "You're welcome. For eliminating this motorcycle and for getting pertinent information for the case."

"You're right." He put his hand on her arm and gave it a rub. "Thank you. But I don't want you to help at the expense of your safety."

She threw up her hands. "Too late."

Yes, it was. There was no closing Pandora's box now. They just had to wait to see what evil they'd unleashed.

She gave a sad chuckle. "My mom says I'm a lodestone for trouble."

No parent should ever say such a thing about their child. Even if it was true.

His mother believed that whatever you spoke over a child made it so, called it into being. For that reason, she only said good things about him and his brothers.

When they were running amok, getting on her nerves, she didn't shout that they were loud, out of control, wild boys who didn't listen. She called them her blessings. Asked them to act like the young self-possessed men that that they were. Even though it took every ounce of her strength to do so.

It worked, too. Every time.

"That's not true. You're not a lodestone for trouble." She was his beacon of hope. A light in the darkness. "You're a good person, trying to do the right thing." He moved his hand to her lower back and ushered her toward her car, wanting to get her out of the cold. "I don't want anything to happen to you." Fate must have been eavesdropping, because she stepped on an icy patch and slipped. "Whoa." He wrapped an arm around her waist, catching her before she fell.

Holden kept his arm there, close and tight around her, until they reached her car.

After she unlocked her door, he opened it for her.

She stood in between the door and the frame, looking up at him. "I already told you, I'm not your responsibility. I'll make it clear to Daniel."

Her long, dark brown hair that didn't know if it wanted to be curly or wavy hung loose. The way he liked it best. Free and wild. Something in her called to him, and the next thing he knew, he was pushing strands from her face back behind her ear. Letting his hand linger, he caressed her cheek.

That instant contact of skin on skin flooded his brain with the memory of kissing her. Something he longed to do again.

This time the way he truly wanted. Leaving no doubt that it was far more than friendly. "And I told you, I don't mind being on the hook. Not where you're concerned."

In fact, he liked having an official reason to look out for her. To camouflage his personal one.

He stroked her skin with the tips of his fingers. Brushed her bottom lip with his thumb. Her mouth had been soft and warm and oh-so-sweet when it had been pressed to his.

Her eyes flashed with heat that sent his thoughts into a tailspin. Rising on the balls of her feet, she leaned over and kissed his cheek. Then she pulled back a little, staying up on her toes, bringing their mouths within a hairsbreadth.

As if testing something.

His resolve? His facade of just friendship?

Sweet Lord, he was going to fail. What he wouldn't give to wrap his arms around her, pull her close and kiss her hard and slow and hungry, the way she deserved.

"Good night," she whispered, searching his eyes.

Her breath was warm on his face, covering him in the scent of peppermint. The moment stretched between them like a physical thing.

He licked his bottom lip, his gaze dropping to her mouth, his resolve on the verge of snapping.

Needing to shatter the moment before he did something he would regret, he stepped back. It took every drop of his willpower. "Drive home safely."

Lowering her head, she got in her car.

He closed the door, gave her roof two knuckle raps and moved away. Watching her drive off, he wondered if he would ever get out from under the relentless pall of shame that hung over him.

For a minute earlier, when Grace was bolstering his spirits and he was staring in her bright eyes, he believed that anything was possible.

That there were still good things in store for him.

Like happiness.

TURNING DOWN OLD MILL ROAD and hitting the gravel that kicked up around the sides of her Chevy, Grace slowed down.

What had she been thinking to lean in so close to Holden's face? That he was going to give her another kiss?

Her heart had stuttered to a near halt as she waited to see what he was going to do. Every cell in her body wanting him to kiss her.

It was so silly.

He only wanted to be friends. And even though she was attracted to him, she needed to spend her free time focusing on school, getting her master's degree. Not fantasizing about Holden. She'd allowed herself to get sidetracked with the wrong guy once before. She didn't want Kevin 2.0, repeating the same mistake.

But Holden wasn't a bad guy. He didn't gamble or

smoke or drink too much, from what she'd seen at Delgado's. And he wasn't violent. It would seem his only vice was misplacing his trust in people who didn't deserve it. This town was putting him through the wringer for it. He was going through a hard time and didn't need her complicating his life.

But when they had been on the side of the road together, all she had wanted was to clear away his pain and fill up the empty spaces with—

High beams flashed on from a vehicle behind her. *What the heck?*

Glancing up at her rearview mirror, she had to squint against the harsh glare. The truck sped up, surging toward her, getting right up on her bumper.

Her pulse kicked up a notch as she dared to press down on the gas pedal. The turnoff to the cottage wasn't far. She just had to get away from this idiot.

Putting distance between them, she took a deep breath. But the truck zipped up behind her again, spraying gravel as it rushed at her. This time the truck bumped the rear of her SUV, giving her car a jolt. The impact caused her seat belt to tighten, cutting into her chest.

She gripped the wheel and floored the accelerator as fear swept through her. Her SUV swerved on the gravel, her tires failing to find traction.

Was that Rodney behind her? Trying to scare her again?

Due to the high beams, she couldn't see the truck clearly.

The driveway of her cottage came up. She made the sharp turn. Loose gravel shifted, slipping out from underneath her tires, causing her to fishtail as she hit the driveway.

The truck kept going, zooming past her.

Pulse hammering in her ears, she managed to straighten out the car and regain control in the driveway. She slammed on the brakes. Taking deep breaths, she tried to steady her nerves.

Thank goodness she was in her Chevy. Out on that gravel road, the Mazda wouldn't have fared too well. She probably would've gone into a spin, might've hit a tree or something. The SUV was older than she was, but it was sturdy and handled well under pressure.

She pulled up in front of the cottage and parked.

Inside the house, she immediately flipped on the lights. Her living room was empty as well as the dining room and kitchen since she had a clear view with the open floor plan. She wasn't surprised.

Rodney couldn't be in two places at once.

She locked the door, putting on the chain, and hung up her coat. This night called for a soak in a warm bubble bath and a large glass of wine. Tomorrow she'd call Holden and tell him about the incident on the road. She went into her bedroom and dropped her purse on the dresser. She tugged off her boots and traipsed into the bathroom. Turning on the light, she noticed something was different. She glanced at her counter.

None of her toiletries had been moved. Her toothbrush was just as she'd left it. But the toilet seat lid was down.

Had she closed it?

This morning her brain had been foggy from the

lack of sleep, and honestly, she couldn't remember, but it wasn't like her to close it.

She opened the lid. With a shriek, she stumbled back in horror, her heart leaping into her throat.

A red snake with white and black stripes hissed up at her from the toilet bowl. Its black, forked tongue flicked in and out of its mouth.

Screaming, she slammed the lid shut. She did *not* want that venomous thing crawling around her house. Her worst nightmare brought to life. She absolutely hated them.

Goose bumps broke out on her arms. Nausea roiled through her right along with the kind of fear she'd never experienced before. She staggered into her bedroom, flipped on the light and leaned against the wall.

Squeezing her eyes shut, she took a shuddering breath, trying to think how best to handle this. Not the issue of Rodney. But the more pressing concern of not being able to use her toilet.

She opened her eyes, trembling all over. Her gaze flew around the room, landing in front of her. She froze as something slithered under the covers of her bed.

Another snake. *Oh, God.* It had to be. She didn't have to see it, but she tugged at the blanket anyway.

Her stomach dropped as bile burned up the back of her throat. The snake uncoiled its red body and slithered in bold relief against the white sheets.

Grace screamed, even though she knew what she'd find. Seeing it still shook her down to her bones. For a split second, she felt something soft and smooth wriggle through her fingers, over her skin. But it was just her imagination.

Shaking her hands, she grabbed her purse and ran. Her heart threatened to beat out of her chest, thundering in her ears. She didn't stop to get her boots. Or her coat. Just ran.

And she kept running until she was out of that house.

Chapter Nine

Holden removed his ringing phone from his pocket. He was pleasantly surprised to see Grace's name on the caller ID.

He was in his truck heading home and put the call through to his Bluetooth. "Hey. Is everything all right?"

"S-s-snakes," Grace said through a shuddering sob.

Was she crying? "What's going on?" he asked, immediately making a U-turn to head to her place.

"In m-m-my house," she said, struggling to speak. "Snakes. Please, help me."

He pressed down on the gas pedal, racing to Old Mill Road. "Okay. Calm down."

Sometimes snakes got in. They were usually looking to get out of the cold or were following prey inside. For a city girl like Grace, it might be startling, but she sounded on the verge of hysterics. "I'm almost there."

Thankfully, he wasn't that far away. He turned onto Old Mill and slowed down only enough to keep traction on the gravel.

"Oh, God," she said, her voice low and quivering.

"Just stay away from it. Better yet, wait for me outside, on the porch."

"I'm...I'm in my car."

Her car?

It wasn't like Grace to overreact, but that seemed excessive.

Pulling into her driveway, he said, "I'm here. See you in a sec." He hung up, putting his phone back in his pocket. Passing her car, he looped around it and stopped next to her Chevy, so that his driver's-side door was beside hers. From his seat, he spotted her, clutching the steering wheel with her forehead pressed down on it.

He cut the engine, climbed down and opened her door. She was trembling all over, completely spooked. When she didn't acknowledge him with a look, concern tightened his gut. He bent over, putting a hand on her back.

She flinched, jerking away from him. Brushing her arms as if something was crawling over her, she stared up at him.

Her eyes were pink from crying. Tears streamed down her cheeks.

He'd never seen her like this. She must've had a phobia of snakes. "Where is it? I'll take care of it."

"There's two." Her bottom lip quivered.

They probably got in together through some hole or crack. "Where did you last see them?"

"In the toilet." She took a deep breath. "And in my bed."

Snakes knew how to slither into some pretty unusual places, but that was the strangest thing he'd ever heard.

"I'll go get them." He closed her car door, to keep

the cold out. Digging in the cargo bed of his truck, he found a thick pair of work gloves. He always had a pair handy from working on the ranch.

Hurrying into the cottage, he left the door cracked. He kept his gaze trained on the floor in case they had made it out from the back of the house and grabbed the poker next to the fireplace.

No sign of either snake as he made his way through the living and dining areas. In the bedroom, the covers had been pulled back, revealing crisp white sheets.

But no snake.

Had she misspoken? Did she mean under her bed?

That would've made much more sense. They liked warm places low to the ground.

He got down on all fours and spotted it slithering across the floor under the frame. Red with black-and-white stripes.

A milk snake.

They looked nasty and venomous and were often confused with copperheads or coral snakes, but they were harmless. You could buy them in larger pet stores or come across them out in the woods with no need to worry.

Still, he tugged on his gloves. Just because the snake's bite wouldn't kill him didn't mean it wouldn't be painful.

Drawing closer to the snake, he distracted it away from his reaching hand with the fire poker. He kept the wrought iron tool low to the hardwood floor and near the snake's head. As soon as the reptile hissed at the poker, striking out at it thinking the object was a potential threat, he used his other hand to gently grab it behind the head.

He held its mouth away so it was unable to snap back at him.

In the bathroom, he went up to the toilet. The lid was closed, but he knew what to expect and got into position.

He flipped the lid up.

A coiled milk snake poked its head out of the bowl. He dangled the tail of the snake in his hand over the toilet as bait. They were cannibals.

It worked like a charm. As the one in the toilet hissed and struck upward, going for the tail, he snatched the other behind the head just like he'd done with the first.

Unaccustomed to the wildlife, discovering them in her home, Grace would've found the situation terrifying.

Holding both snakes, he stalked out of the house. He headed off the porch, passing the stump and ax she used to chop firewood, and carted them over to the trees. He tossed the snakes, releasing them back where they belonged. Making his way to the Chevy, he removed the gloves and stuffed them in his jacket pocket.

He opened her door and peered in. "No more snakes. I got rid of them."

She looked up at him. "Did you kill them?"

"No. I turned them loose outside."

Her features tensed in horror. "Why?"

"They're not venomous."

"Are you sure?" she asked, her voice pitching higher. "They looked dangerous. Deadly."

"I'm positive. There are only two poisonous snakes in Wyoming. The prairie rattlesnake and the midget faded rattler. Trust me, if you come across either of those, you'll know the difference. The ones in your house were milk snakes. They're good to have on the property. They'll eat rodents and other pests, keeping them from getting in the house."

She dropped her head in her hands. "I'm not worried about mice. Those I can handle. I just don't want those things back in the house."

"Come on." He held out a hand to help her out. She took it, her warm fingers curling around his, and stepped out. His gaze dropped to her feet. She was only wearing socks. Not even a coat. "Where are your boots?"

"Inside," she said, sounding overwhelmed.

He scooped her up in his arms and braced for her to protest.

Surprisingly, she didn't. Grace wrapped her arms around his neck and rested her head on his shoulder. She was soft and warm and light in his arms.

And part of him didn't ever want to let her go.

He carried her inside and set her down on the sofa. "I'll look around for any holes and cracks, any possible entry points for how they got in." At least one of them anyway.

The snake in the toilet probably got in through the ventilation pipes on the roof. Since bathroom plumbing was connected, it could've slithered its way through the system and into her john. It was more likely to happen in the summer when the reptiles were looking for a cool place out of the heat. Still, so odd that they had both gotten in on the same night and in such eerie spots.

It was enough to creep anyone out.

"There's no need to search for entry points. Rodney Owens put them in there."

Rocking back on his heels, he put his hands on his hips. "Why would he do that?"

That question dried up her tears and lit a fire in her eyes. "Because he's a sick jerk who's trying to scare me into breaking my lease. He did a heck of a job tonight. Putting one in my toilet and another in my bed. The audacity of it."

"It wasn't on the floor?"

"No. It was in between the sheets. That SOB had the nerve to even make the bed back up."

"Tell me what's been going on," he demanded.

She unloaded the whole story she'd hidden from him. How Rodney had started harassing her after she moved in, and had been crowding her space, trying to intimidate her for months. But it wasn't until yesterday that his empty threats had taken a vicious turn. First, waiting for her in the dark. Then slashing her tires. Now this. Damn snakes.

Grace was lucky this time. It had only been harmless snakes. But what about next time?

When she was finished, Holden was shaking with anger. He took a steady breath, trying to calm down, but he was livid. "Is that everything?"

"Someone hit the rear of my car with their truck tonight. On Old Mill. It was deliberate. They had on high beams, kept bearing down on me. Trying to scare me. I couldn't see who it was, but I think it might have been Rodney."

His chest squeezed. His hands clenched at his sides, his temples throbbing, he wanted to rip Rodney apart. "I'm going to go put a stop to it."

There wasn't going to be a next time. Not on his watch.

He turned on his heel for the door.

Grace jumped up and caught his arm. "Please don't leave me alone." She glanced toward her bedroom. "I can't be here by myself just yet."

"Grab some things. You can stay with me on the ranch."

"I can't." She shook her head. "I *won't* let him win by running me out of here. Not even for a single night," she said through gritted teeth.

Grace had lost the battle tonight with the snakes, but she wasn't ready to concede the war with Rodney. That was the woman he knew and admired, and he would expect nothing less from her. Even if digging her heels in only complicated things.

Holden keyed his radio on his shoulder since he was still in uniform. "This is Chief Deputy Powell."

"Dispatch here," Livingston responded.

"I need someone to go to Rodney Owens's place and question him." Holden listed the things that Grace had experienced. "If he's not home, find him. Rattle him a little. If he gives you any legal reason, haul him in and lock him up. Provided that fails, give him a warning." Either way, Holden would speak with Rodney tomorrow and set him straight. This harassment was going to end.

"Roger. We'll make it happen. Hang on a sec. Ashley's back and wants to speak to you."

After a brief delay, she got on the radio. "I spoke with Ruby Belle. She confirmed Jared's story about Emma's visit. Do you want me to cut him loose?"

"Yeah. Give him our apologies about the delay. Blame it on forensics with his bike. Good work. See you tomorrow."

"Get some sleep," Ashley said before disconnecting.

Holden looked at Grace. "After the holidays, do you mind if I contact a security person my family deals with to see about him putting up cameras?"

"Sure. Thank you."

"Do you want me to stay the night? I could sleep on the sofa." He'd be cramped on the worn-out love seat, and in the morning, his neck would be stiff and his back would ache, but he'd do it without complaint.

"I could really use the company tonight."

"Show me where you keep your linen."

She took him into the bedroom and opened the bottom drawer of the bureau. There were stacks of neatly folded sheets and blankets. "I appreciate you doing this. I'm sorry—"

"Nope. Remember what I told you, no apologies," he said, cutting her off, and she nodded. "I know this will be hard, but you should take a warm shower and unwind so you can get some sleep. I'll only be a scream away."

"I'll try." She went to the doorway of the bathroom and hesitated.

He could imagine what she was feeling. Anger. Embarrassment. Fear. Naked vulnerability that had forced her to call him for help. Something she never would've done unless she had no other choice.

All of her emotions were justified. He would do everything possible to ensure Rodney's terrorism stopped. In the meantime, he'd work on getting her to feel better.

Taking a deep breath, Grace stepped inside the bathroom and shut the door. After a minute or two, the shower started running.

Holden stripped the bed, put fresh linen on for her, and tossed the stuff tainted by the snake into the washing machine. Then he made up the sofa with a sheet and blanket.

Sometimes he kept a clean uniform in his truck for emergencies. Not today.

It figures.

There was no telling how long it would take Grace to fall asleep, which meant he had no idea how much shut-eye he'd get. In the morning, he wouldn't want to waste time running home to change.

He took out his cell and texted his mom. She had to come near here on her way into town and could drop off what he needed.

"You made the bed," Grace said.

Spinning around, he faced her. She stood in the doorway of her bedroom wearing a pale blue nightgown made of stretchy cotton that hugged her upper body and fell to a line of lace at the hem just above her knees. Her was face clean, her skin radiant, and her eyes were weary. She had warm woolen socks on her feet.

"I thought new sheets might help." His phone dinged, and he looked at the screen to find a text from his mom.

No problem. See you around 10. Love you, sweetie.

"Is everything all right?" Grace asked. "Do you have to leave?" The worry on her beautiful face tugged at his heart.

"Everything is fine. I'm all yours tonight."

"Good." She gave him a small, sad smile. "Can I ask another favor?"

"Name it."

Her gaze bounced to her bedroom and then back to him. "Would you sleep with me?"

"I, um, well…" The question had caught him so off guard it had reduced him to stammering.

"I didn't mean sex," she said, stumbling over the words. "The thought of getting into bed and closing my eyes has me on the verge of breaking into a cold sweat. Would you mind," she said, lowering her head and biting her bottom lip, "getting in the bed with me? I understand if sleeping with me is too weird, but at least hold me until I fall asleep?" Her voice was tight and strained like it was the most difficult thing in the world for her to ask. She was strong and vibrant even as she was also delicate and shy.

"The only way I'll share a bed and sleep with you is if you twist my arm and make me."

Her smile widened, and his heart jumped.

He joined her in the bedroom. "Would you give me a minute to freshen up?" His first opportunity to get physically close to her was on the heels of a sixteen-hour workday.

Perfect.

"Sure." She stood in the corner with her back pressed to the wall, where she had sight of the bed and both doors.

With her being so unnerved, he could understand her caution.

In the bathroom, he didn't take too long washing his hands, cleaning his face, neck and a few other parts in the sink. He would've killed for a shower, but he didn't have anything to change into. It would have to wait until tomorrow.

Stepping back in the bedroom, he had already taken off everything above the waist except for his white cotton tank top. He removed his utility belt with holstered gun and set it on her dresser. Then he unlaced his boots and pulled them off along with his socks and put it all to the side.

"Would you get in first?" she asked, and he did.

It was a full-size bed, not leaving a lot of space.

"Do you mind if I keep the lamp on?" she asked.

He had anticipated that she would want to. "I can sleep with anything on, the light, the TV, radio, through someone else snoring. You name it." He extended his arm, waiting for her.

"Wow." She jumped in under the covers with the urgency and determination of someone yanking off a Band-Aid.

He let her decide how close to get, and she snuggled up right on him, bringing a smile to his face. Her sweet, seductive scent tantalized and tormented him, sending his thoughts on a tangent. She always smelled the same, but this was the first time he'd gotten to inhale it up close. Something floral and familiar. It made him think of a summer's day bright with sunshine, filled with laughter and warmth. The elusive source struck him.

Peonies.

She smelled like peonies.

"I was like that as a child, too," he said, wrapping his arms around her and taking another deep whiff. "My mom used to call me her easy baby."

"Really, when did she stop?"

"Uh, right after the scandal with Renee and Jim."

She laughed, as he had hoped. Talking and laughter were sometimes the best cure.

"Are you serious?" she asked, her tone ten times lighter.

"Unfortunately, I am. All my other brothers gave Mom and Dad a hard time in some way. With five of us, I stood out for being easy." He was the second-born son with the same pressures as the first. "She was in labor with me for only two hours. No epidural needed. Said I slid right out. I was an excellent eater. The best sleeper. Got good grades. Followed the rules. Athletic."

Everything in his life had come easily. Everything except love. He'd never had any luck in that department.

"High school quarterback selected all-state," she said.

"You were actually listening and not using me for free pie." He tickled her side.

She squirmed, rubbing her warm, soft body against

him, teasing his senses in every way possible. None of them good, but yet they were.

Her physique was lean, dainty, but not so much that she didn't still have the swell at her hips, the feminine curves that made his mouth water.

"I pay close attention to everything you tell me." Her admission was sincere and warmed him from the inside out. "I can see you've kept in tiptop shape." She feathered a hand across his chest.

Long-fought yearning flooded through him. He clenched his jaw against it, straining to think of something to say that didn't have anything to do with his body. Or hers, or how good she felt snuggled up so close. "Unlike everyone else, I think my dad was relieved when the scandal happened."

"Why?" she asked, burrowing closer, sliding her palm over his neck into his hair, slipping her leg over his.

Every little movement from her fed that gnawing hunger inside him. Swallowing, he was so damn hard now he ached with every heartbeat.

So he kept talking. To distract her and himself. "Well, all of his sons followed after the maternal line in terms of careers. Law enforcement, the lot of us. Every time a generation of the Powell line gets only boys it's a bit of a jinx. Because none of them want to work on the ranch. That's how it starts. But eventually, something draws or forces one to abandon their other pursuits and take over the Shooting Star."

"Was it like that for your dad?"

"Yep. He was one of three boys. With the scandal, he thought it was a sign."

"That it would make you leave the sheriff's department and take over the ranch."

It was the first time his father had looked at him with disappointment when that didn't happen. "Yes, but it'll be one of my brothers. Not me."

That wasn't his destiny. He was a rancher and always would be. It was in his blood. But he was also a lawman and refused to give up his career as one.

"If you'd left the sheriff's department, we would've never met." She tipped her head back, meeting his eyes.

The air heated, thickening between them. The whole of her was everything he craved and worried about at the same time.

"Oh, we would've met." Somehow. Someway. And he would have been struck by her beauty and her smile. Turned inside out by the hot desire he felt whenever he looked at her. Only he wouldn't have had to worry about upsetting his boss by getting involved with her. "What's meant to be, will be."

He ran his hand down her spine to her lower back. She shivered in his arms, keeping her gaze locked to his. Her thigh slid closer to his crotch. So close that it erased any doubt in his mind that she could feel how much he wanted her.

Desire crackled like invisible lightning. He tried to ignore it and failed. Catching her chin and lifting her head, he crushed his mouth to hers. It wasn't hesitant or slow, but insistent and demanding.

She pressed flush against him, deepening the kiss.

Tangling his hand in her hair, he lost himself in the taste of her, the feel of her slender body. Holding her close, kissing her, thinking about making love to her, woke something inside him, bringing him back to life.

She brightened his world. Gave him hope.

But she had reached out to him at a vulnerable time. He wouldn't take advantage of that.

Reluctantly, he pulled his mouth from hers.

"Holden," she whispered, putting a hand between them, her palm to his chest. "We can't—"

"I know." This feeling of falling for someone was the worst.

The adrenaline and electricity that flared whenever she was near was turning into a form of torture. There was nothing more that he would like to do than kiss Grace again, strip her naked and make love to her. But he had a laundry list of reasons as to why that would be a bad idea.

Apparently, she had reasons of her own as well.

"Was that supposed to be just friendly, like earlier?" she asked.

He didn't want to lie or hide the truth. "No."

"I didn't know," she said. "I mean, I wasn't sure."

"Of what?"

"If you had feelings for me." She searched his eyes. "Romantic feelings."

How could she have not known. Sure, he had downplayed the meaning of their first kiss, but he would've sworn his overtures had been obvious. All the time he'd spent hanging around her. Making any excuse to touch her, even in a casual way, like taking a dish from her hand in the restaurant before she could set it down in front of him so that their fingers grazed. He took every opportunity to brush crumbs from her face, even when there were none. In the last few months, he'd eaten so much pie at Delgado's that his uniform had gotten tight.

"I thought you were always so nice to me because I'm Daniel's sister and you wanted to get in good with him."

She thought he'd been brownnosing instead of flirting. Wow. He was really off his game.

"And then," she added, "you told me that the kiss on the side of the road was platonic."

"I never used that word." Not once had he ever looked at or thought about Grace in a platonic way. And he never would. "But I shouldn't have crossed the line."

"We crossed it together. I kissed you back. Because I have feelings for you, too," she said, and his heart swelled. "Which is the problem."

Just like that it deflated. "I'm not following."

"Part of the reason I moved out here was to focus. On my master's degree. On finding my center. On remembering what makes me happy. I got distracted once, by a guy, who turned out to be wrong for me. I don't want to get sidetracked again."

He didn't want to derail her from her goals or hold her back.

Maybe in time, once she'd gotten her degree and he'd proven himself to Daniel, repaired his reputation, they might be able to explore the possibility of something more.

Falling in love was more than the urgency of desire. A relationship with her would be worth the wait.

"I should go to the sofa," he said, sitting up.

But she stopped him from leaving. "I hate to do this

to you, but can you wait until I fall asleep? Unless it's too much to ask."

If it was something Grace needed, it would never be too much.

He pressed a kiss to her forehead and brought her back into his arms. "It's no problem."

Chapter Ten

The buzzing woke Grace. Her phone vibrated, ringing on silent, on the dresser.

She opened her eyes to the most beautiful sight. Holden sound asleep on her bed, his arms still wrapped around her. Captivated by him, she let the phone go to voice mail.

She wanted to touch him all over. But she didn't, steeling herself against the desire, against the sight of him, long and powerful like a lion. She wondered what he did to keep up the tan, the sculpted muscles, what he looked like shaving in the morning.

That kiss last night. It had been everything. Explosive, full of hunger and longing. He'd been demanding, as a lover would be, yet he'd also been tender. She didn't know a kiss could be like that.

He was such a good guy. Not only that but he was the first man, ever, who she wanted to give herself to without holding anything back.

And that scared her. Made her want to run in the opposite direction.

Part of her wondered if it had been a mistake to push him away last night. But she hated what a fool she'd been with Kevin, that she'd been so blind to who he really was. How desperately she'd wanted to be loved, so desperate that she hadn't put a stop to his emotional abuse until his grandmother, her palliative patient she'd cared for the past two years, had told her the truth about his gambling and begged her to stay away from him.

That was when Grace had realized that Kevin hadn't really been interested in her. Instead, he'd had grand hopes of getting his hands on Selene's fortune through her. All addicts would do anything to get their fix.

It had been a wake-up call in more ways than one.

Speaking of which. The phone buzzed again on the dresser. Whoever was calling was persistent.

Grace slid out from under Holden's arm, not wanting to disturb him just yet. He'd told her stories about his childhood and growing up on the Shooting Star ranch until she'd fallen asleep. He needed the rest.

She tiptoed across the floor, grabbed the phone and shut the door as she stepped out of the room. Walking into the kitchen to start coffee, she glanced at the screen.

It was her mother.

With a groan, she contemplated letting it go to voice mail once more. But she had promised. "Morning, Mom." Holding the phone between her ear and shoulder, she turned on the faucet and filled the pot with water.

"I just finished doing yoga with my instructor, Florian, out on the patio by the pool overlooking the ocean, and I thought of you, Bug."

Rub in the fact that I'm freezing and miss the ocean.

Grace looked through the window in front of the

kitchen sink. The thing that made her fall in love with this cottage, besides the cheap rent and the fact it was furnished, was the incredible view of Medicine Bow Peak. Sometimes she felt a little isolated out here, but it was peaceful and beautiful. The cottage was her sanctuary.

"Well, I'm making coffee with a breathtaking view of the mountains."

"Nothing like the Santa Monica Mountains, I'm sure," her mom said, which Selene also had a view of. "But you've never been much for hiking, have you?"

Rolling her eyes, Grace put grinds in the filter and hit the start button. "I came here to discover myself and try new things. For a change of scenery. A different way of life."

She could finally breathe. It had taken a month to settle in—fix the place up a bit to make it habitable, get a new car better suited for the weather she'd encountered and learn how to chop her own firewood. A feat she didn't think she would be able to accomplish until Daniel had introduced her to an essential tool—a wood splitter. Once she got the hang of the job at Delgado's and began taking classes at the University of Wyoming, she'd started to like herself again.

Love herself in a way she never had before. With no need for anyone else's approval.

Moving to Laramie was the best decision she had ever made.

"Is that why you're throwing away the nursing degree

I paid for by being a waitress?" Selene made a distinct sound that was a mix of disgust and disappointment.

Grace knew it very well.

"I'm taking a break. Caring for Miss Linda took a toll." Kevin's grandmother had been an extraordinary woman. Grace had grown close to her. Losing her to cystic fibrosis had broken her heart. But not Kevin's. The man probably didn't have one. "And I'm working on an advanced degree, which I'm paying for. Please don't start this again. I don't want to fight with you."

"Fine, fine." Her mother sighed. "You must be so lonely out there," Selene said, deciding on a new angle of attack. "Come home. Just for the holidays. We could go to Napa Valley. Like we did for your twenty-second birthday. We had so much fun. Remember?"

Great food. Even better wine. It had been a fantastic trip…when Selene wasn't talking. But of course her mother always had something to say. "I remember."

"And before you say no, guess who's been asking about you nonstop?"

"Who?" she asked, yawning and stretching.

"Kevin," her mother said, brightly. "He keeps calling me because you've blocked his number or something."

Any other parent would've taken that as a hint not to bring up their ex. "Yes, for a reason." She had changed her phone number, but Selene had given him the new one.

Why was he suddenly being so persistent, after months of silence?

It didn't make any sense. Kevin hadn't been so much devastated when she broke up with him as he had been annoyed. She had ruined his scheme to get to Selene's money, forcing him to start over and find another easy mark.

The coffee maker beeped that it was done. She grabbed two mugs, setting one out for Holden, and poured herself a hot cup.

"I think you should at least hear what he has to say," her mom said. "Kevin told me that he's willing to do anything to make things right, to make you happy. And I told him a grand gesture is required."

Grace nearly choked on her coffee. "Narcissists don't know how to love, much less make someone else happy." A knock sounded at the door. "I've got to go, Mom. Someone's here."

"If you come for Christmas, I'll get you a diamond tennis bracelet, just like the one I have." Selene was bringing out the big guns. Bribery with jewelry. "You always admire it when I wear it."

"Because the bling is mesmerizing." Grace walked toward the door, carrying her coffee. "Looking at it, I know how a cat feels when they see something shiny. I appreciate the offer of such an extravagant gift." Such gestures were only made when Selene was feeling desperate. "But what am I going to do with an eight-carat tennis bracelet in the *wilderness*? Use it to blind a bear? Bye. Love you."

She thumbed the disconnect button and opened the door.

"Morning." A stunning woman in her late fifties, maybe early sixties, stood beaming at her. She had golden blond hair, eyes the color of the midday sky and glow-ing skin. "I'm Holly." She swept up to the threshold, giving her a hug.

Her perfume enveloped Grace. Powdery wildflowers and musk. It smelled of money.

Grace was well acquainted with the scent.

Holly breezed inside. "You must be Grace. It's such a pleasure to finally meet you."

Grace closed the door, stunned into silence. Clearly this woman knew who she was. Grace only wished the familiarity hadn't been one-sided. "I'm sorry, Holly, but who exactly are you?"

Her smile faltered and fell. "Oh, heavens. Holden didn't tell you I was dropping by."

Then it hit Grace. The hair. The striking eyes. The smooth, tanned skin. "You're Holden's mother?"

"In the flesh." The smile resurfaced.

"I should've realized. He looks so much like you."

The bedroom door opened.

"Yes, at least I have one son that favors me," Holly said.

"Hey, Mom." Holden came out of the bedroom, scratching his head. "That's not true. Logan looks like you, too."

"I meant not only in looks but also temperament." Holly chuckled. "Holden is the only one. All the others favor their father, Buck, in one way or another." She handed Holden the garment bag that was draped over her arm. "Here are your things. Toiletries are at the bottom. I was just telling Grace how nice it is to finally meet your girlfriend. It's about time you got back on that saddle."

Holden stiffened, his eyes widening. "No, no, Mom. Grace isn't my girlfriend. We're only friends."

"Really? You could've fooled me." Holly looked at the made-up sofa that hadn't been slept in and then her gaze bounced to Grace's nightgown and Holden's bare feet. "Where are your boots? And firearm?"

They were back in the bedroom. Which was not going to give the right impression.

"Thanks for getting my things," Holden said, not answering the question.

"Of course, sweetie." Holly turned to Grace. "Excuse my assumption, regardless of how close to the truth it might be, considering you two are sleeping together. For someone who isn't his girlfriend, he sure does talk about you all the time."

Grace's cheeks flushed hot as she tensed. "What?"

"Mom," Holden snapped as his face tightened into one of those expressions that kids threw at their parents who were embarrassing them.

Holly raised her palms. "Okay, it's not *all* the time. Just a lot."

"You talk about me?" Grace's voice was a whisper. She was surprised she could speak at all.

When he didn't respond, his mother leaned in close and put a hand on her shoulder. The scent of her exquisite perfume curled around her in a sweet caress.

"All good things," Holly said. "I promise. He has never spoken about a woman the way he talks about you. Never. I've been so happy that he found someone so pretty and smart and compassionate."

The pretty and smart part was nice, but he thought she was compassionate?

"Is that coffee I smell?" Holden asked, heading toward the kitchen.

Grace stared at him in disbelief. In awe. "I just brewed some. Would you like a cup, Mrs. Powell?" Where were her manners?

"Call me Holly, and no, thank you. My work here is done." Flashing another smile worthy of a toothpaste commercial, she waltzed to the door.

"And you're wrong, Mom," Holden said from the kitchen, pouring himself coffee. "I only slept in the same bed with her because she was terrified of the snakes. But we did not sleep together."

"Not yet," Holly said. "It'll happen. I'm never wrong about these things. And what snakes?"

"Rodney Owens put one in my toilet and another in my bed," Grace said, shivering at the memory.

"Rattlers?" his mother asked with alarm.

"No," Holden said. "Milk snakes."

A confused expression crossed Holly's face. "Why on earth would he do such a thing?"

Grace quickly explained, but it took longer than she had hoped.

"My word." Holly turned to her son, giving him a look that could peel paint. "You better put that boy in his place and see to it that he leaves her alone."

"Yes, ma'am." Holden took a sip from his mug. "I'm all over it."

"Rodney's father, Oscar, is a weak man," Holly said. "Ever since the mother passed, that boy has been like a rabid junkyard dog off a leash. What he's been doing to you is terrible." She gave Grace another hug. "Please don't take this the wrong way, honey, but may I ask why you chose to live here?" Holly looked around at the rustic, run-down condition of the place. "Instead of accepting your brother's offer to stay with him on his farm."

It was no exaggeration on Holly's part that Holden had told his mother quite a lot. The only reason his mom didn't already know the answer to the question was because Holden had never asked, and Grace had never volunteered to share the reason.

"Daniel and I aren't close," Grace said. "He's twelve years older. By the time I was six, he was out of the house." And had abandoned her to Selene. In many ways, she'd grown up feeling like only child. "He's always acted more like a father figure than a brother who wants to be my friend." He loved her and she him, but they were never going to be bosom buddies. "I left California for a fresh start, on my own terms. This cottage is a far cry from being five-star luxury accommodations." Which she could have in a heartbeat, if she only sold her soul to her mother. "But this rental is mine and I don't have to depend on anyone for it."

Despite its shortcomings, the cottage had a charm of its own. It was cozy and more comfortable since she'd painted, and she loved the large wood beams on the ceiling throughout.

"I admire you for sticking to your guns. As well as your independence." Holly grabbed the doorknob but hesitated. "Do you have plans for Christmas Eve?"

"Uh, no," Grace said, caught off guard. "I don't."

"Well, you do now. You will be at our house." Holly opened the door and walked down the stairs to a gleaming Hummer.

Was Holden's family rich?

He had never said a word about money. Not even when she had told him about Selene's lavish lifestyle, being born with a silver spoon, and the pressure of growing up in the Pacific Palisades, where everything revolved around status, power and the almighty dollar.

Panic flared in Grace. She shivered from the cold breeze and the prospect of a swanky event. "Will there be a lot of people? Is it going to be fancy? Do I have to dress up?"

Gowns and heels were her worst nightmare.

Second only to snakes.

"Honey, you can wear a burlap sack," Holly said. "We do not put on airs. It's about coming together and having a good time. Only family. And close *friends*." Grinning, Holly waved. "See you tomorrow night."

The weekend had sneaked up on her. She couldn't believe today was Saturday and tomorrow was Christmas Eve.

Grace waved and closed the door. She turned around to find Holden staring at her.

Heat washed through her again, along with a tremor of excitement.

"I'm sorry about my mother," he said. "She likes to stir the pot. Always thinks she's right."

"I thought we don't do apologies."

He grinned. "Always let a man apologize to a woman. We don't do it nearly enough. Or so my father says."

Setting his coffee down, he drew closer. "I'm sorry if she made you uncomfortable."

Sometimes having your eyes opened was a necessary discomfort. She had no idea that Holden was genuinely interested in her, for no other reason than he liked her. A lot.

"It's nice that you're close to your mother. That you can talk to her about anything, and she actually listens, tries to make you feel better."

"I take it things aren't like that with *Selene*." He did jazz hands as he uttered her name.

Laughing, she shook her head. She had described her mother vividly. Mostly to see if he was impressed by the fact that her mom had been a supermodel or if he wanted to hear more about the woman men drooled over rather than learning more about her. It wouldn't have been the first time she'd experienced such humiliation. Sometimes guys had dated her simply because of who her mother was and not because they liked Grace at all.

But Holden didn't care that her mother was wealthy and famous. None of it had fazed him.

Now Holly had confirmed it. Proof it wasn't her mother, or Selene's fortune, or even that she was Daniel's sister that attracted him to her and had him talking about her *all the time*.

The feeling was…odd.

"Not even close," Grace said. "Let's just say she's the number one reason why I left California."

He reached out and rubbed her bare arms, making her skin tingle. "If you had to leave the third largest state, then it's pretty bad."

She laughed harder this time.

How did he do it? Always find a way to bring a smile to her face, to lift her spirits, even when things were darkest?

She wanted to pull him close, hug him, hold him. As a thank-you, for having that gift and sharing it with her. And if she was being honest, also as something more.

Let it happen, she told herself. But then came that inner voice of warning.

Don't be a fool.

Why did that voice sound like her mother's?

Holden was striking and strong and so sexual. She would be setting herself up for a gigantic fall.

One of the good things about Selene was that she had forbidden Grace from ever reading fairy tales or watching animated films about princesses. Her mother said it misled women into believing in happily-ever-after, when there was no such thing.

His cell phone rang. He dropped his hand, taking the cell from his pocket, and answered. "Yep." After listening for a minute, he said, "Good. I'll be there shortly." He hung up. "We've got Rodney in custody. Locked up in the drunk tank. Livingston found him at one thirty this morning in a bar. Not only was he bragging about what he did to you, but he also took a swing at Livingston." His hand balled into a fist at his side.

She didn't think she'd ever seen Holden look so hard or so cold. "What are you going to do?"

"Exactly what my mother told me to. Put him in his place. And when I'm done, he's never going to bother you again."

Chapter Eleven

Holden had taken his time driving to the sheriff's office because he wanted to be in full control when he spoke to Rodney. Not unhinged to the point he unlocked the cell and gave Rodney a reason to press charges against him.

Even if the man might deserve the beatdown he wanted to give him.

He arrived. He waited. He calmed down. Ate breakfast. Sifted through the piles of paperwork on his desk. Started his report on Jared Simpson.

Holden was still waiting on Emma's medical records. It was the only official way to see if Gary might have ever abused his daughter. But there was another angle to see if the Burks had a history of violence that extended beyond Emma that Holden hadn't yet explored.

Grabbing his landline, he phoned the hospital. "Chief Deputy Holden from the sheriff's office. I'd like to speak with Nurse Terri Tipton."

"Terri is off today. She'll be back tomorrow afternoon. Is there anything I can help you with?"

A nurse who didn't know him, much less trust him, wouldn't be willing to talk off the record and disclose information that was protected by HIPAA. Anything he learned without a subpoena was inadmissible, but he just needed to know if he was barking up the wrong tree.

"My office submitted a request for medical records on a deceased victim, Emma Burk. Do you have any idea when they'll be ready?" Holden asked.

"One minute while I look that up for you." After a pause, she spoke again. "I see it here in the system. Since you wanted us to go as far back as possible, it's taking some time, but they should be available for pickup tomorrow."

"Great. Can you ask Terri to call me when they're ready? I needed to speak to her in person and I'd like to kill two birds with one stone."

"Sure. No problem. I'll make a note in the system."

As he hung up and looked back at his report, something Jared had said gave him an idea. He left his office and went into the open space where all the other deputies worked. Ashley wasn't in yet, so he headed for the next best choice.

"Hey, Mitch," he said, "something has been bugging me."

"What's that?" Deputy Cody asked, spinning in his seat to face him. Not only was he one of their newest recruits, but he was also their only helicopter pilot.

"How Emma Burk got a lift back to the B and B. Somebody drove her there because she didn't have time to walk. It's possible Todd went looking for her after Jared called him and he found her on the road. Gave her a lift, thinking he'd talk to her, and they ended up fighting. But what if she called him for a ride? Or someone else? She knew a lot of people. Some of them shady. There might be someone else with a motive to kill her if they knew she was about to divulge their business to McCoy next month."

"But Starlights don't have money for cell phones. How would she call someone for a lift?"

"Exactly, and she didn't use Jared's phone to call anyone."

"So, what are you thinking?"

"I want you to see what pay phones are in service between Jared's place and say the halfway point to the B and B on any routes she might've walked." There were fewer than a hundred working pay phones in the state, but at least a quarter of those were scattered about town. "When you pinpoint the ones that she could've possibly used, I want you to see if any nearby place has any surveillance footage available to look at."

"Sure, no problem."

"And when Ashley gets in," Holden said, "update her on everything and have her help out."

Mitch gave a nod and got to work.

With his blood pressure back to normal, Holden strode down the hall to the holding cell where Rodney Owens was locked up.

Holden clanged a metal baton against the bars of the cell, rousing Rodney from his drunken stupor. "Get up!"

Rodney jolted upright on the bench, looking around, wild-eyed and drowsy. "What's going on?" He wiped drool from his mouth with the back of his hand.

"Heard you had a little fun last night at Grace Clark's place?"

"Yeah." Dragging a hand over his red face, Rodney chuckled. "I showed that city gal. Bet I scared the bejesus out of her. Only wish I could've been there to see it. Or better yet, had a video camera set up so I could play it back. In slow motion. Over and over. Maybe put a soundtrack to it." He laughed harder, so pleased with himself. "Put it on the internet."

Holden clenched his jaw. "You could've scared her to death."

"Oh, come on." Rodney waved a hand at him. "It was a harmless prank."

"Slashing her tires and trying to run her off the road wasn't harmless. She could've gone into a spin and hit a tree."

"Huh?" Rodney climbed to his feet and staggered closer. "What are you talking about? I didn't try to run her off the road. Or slash her tires."

Holden considered him for a moment, trying to decide if he believed him. "But you waited for her inside the cottage, in the dark, on Thursday night, and you also put the snakes in her toilet and her bed last night?"

Chuckling again, Rodney nodded. "Yeah. That last one was really good, right?"

Holden smacked the bars with the baton, the strident sound making Rodney flinch. "What if she had a heart condition or epilepsy and had a seizure? Or fainted and hit her head? You could've killed her."

"I didn't think of that." Scowling, he gave a one-shoulder shrug. "I searched her medicine cabinet, but I didn't find any prescriptions. I wasn't trying to kill her. I just want her to leave." A wicked grin tugged at his mouth. "Guess I got to think of something even better next time," he said, snickering.

"Listen to me, there won't be a next time and she isn't leaving. She's going to stay right there in that cottage until her lease ends. And if your father renews it, then she'll be there longer."

Humor drained from Rodney's face. His features twisted. His bloodshot eyes narrowed. He looked like something that had crawled out of the bowels of hell.

But what Rodney didn't know was that Holden had enough fury in his belly to wrestle the devil himself and win.

"That is my place!" Rodney bellowed, grabbing hold of the bars. "My daddy was supposed to sell it after my mother died. And now he can't because of Grace Clark. Outsider meddling in other folks' business. Nobody else was stupid enough to get in the middle of a family squabble and rent the cottage."

"She didn't know what was going on between you two. She is not the one you should be upset with. Your father chose to rent it rather than sell it and give you a dime, you dim-witted bully."

"Dim-witted? I was smart enough to get the better of her twice." Rodney held up two fingers. "Ha, ha. She's the dim-witted one. Probably screamed her head off thinking those snakes could kill her."

Rodney was lucky that there were bars separating them and Holden was wearing a uniform, sworn to uphold the law, otherwise he would knock some sense into him.

"You're such a genius," Holden said, "that you confessed to illegal entry and harassment."

"So what? I won't do jail time for it. She can't stop me. Nobody can."

This time Holden smiled. "You're not above the law. She's going to file charges against you. After she does and you're convicted, then she's going to get an injunction from the court to stop this behavior."

Grace didn't know it yet, but Holden would see to it that she did so.

"What's an injunction?" Rodney asked.

"Your lawyer will explain it to you. Bottom line, you violate it, and you will do jail time. To give you a little taste of what you have to look forward to, you'll be spending the weekend in that cell."

"You can't do that to me!"

"Oh, but I can. In fact, I'm already doing it."

"Why are you taking her side? Her brother stole the job you were supposed to get. You should be sheriff. Not him."

How ironic that he was the one person in town who thought so. But Holden suspected Rodney was only saying what he thought Holden wanted to hear.

"You should know that Grace has me and the entire Powell clan on her side." Holden put his fists on his hips. "Mess with her, you mess with us. Got it?"

Rodney shrank back, understanding what the Powell name meant. Holden's family had been there for generations, had power and money to back it up, held sway over many, many things, and could make life difficult for a troublemaker like Rodney.

But throwing that kind of weight around was never done lightly and only when absolutely necessary.

"I—I—I didn't know," Rodney stammered, and Holden enjoyed seeing the fear in his eyes after what he'd put Grace through. "I'll lay off. I can wait until June. Or whenever she decides to leave."

"Now that you do know, you're going to spend the weekend drafting an apology letter to her, which I will deliver personally. If you write a sincere one with good penmanship—I don't want to see any words misspelled or crossed out—" he wagged a finger "—no matter how long it takes you to get it right, then you can spend Christmas at home. If you don't, you'll sit here through the holiday, and on Tuesday you'll appear before a judge along with a public defender or attorney of your choosing to discuss your charges, including drunk and disorderly conduct and assaulting a law enforcement officer."

Rodney sobered right up. "I'll write the letter."

"Happy to hear that we could see eye to eye on this. You are not to do repairs on her house or enter it anymore."

"But my dad is too old to do it and we can't afford to hire someone."

"If she submits a request for maintenance, you will call me, and I'll see that it's taken care of."

"Okay." Rodney nodded vigorously with full understanding and willingness to comply.

"There's one more thing. Are you sure you didn't slash her tires or run her off the road?"

"No," Rodney said, his eyes bulging from his head, "it wasn't me. I swear it on my mother's grave. I only did stupid, harmless stuff. I mean stuff that I thought was harmless. I didn't think about the possibility of a heart condition or epilepsy."

Holden believed him. "All right."

"I can start working on that letter right now, if you'd like."

"I'll make sure Deputy Cody gets you a pad and pen." Holden stalked off to call Grace.

If Rodney hadn't run her off the road or slashed her tires, then who in the hell had?

"WHAT ON EARTH is going on?" Xavier asked Grace in a rough whisper behind the bar as two more Iron Warriors strode into Delgado's.

Grace's mouth went dry.

They had been showing up in dribs and drabs, two or three at a time, the roar of motorcycles heralding their arrival, since she got there. Like they had a lookout to call them and say when to start.

None of them had ordered anything. They said they were waiting on the *rest* to arrive. By now, there were fifteen or twenty stone-faced Iron Warriors in the bar and grill.

Most of their patrons had cleared out as if they were anticipating trouble.

She was starting to wonder if she should've left, too, but she had a sneaking suspicion that they only would have followed, because they were there for her.

"I may have attracted some unwanted attention," she said to Xavier.

Another growling motorcycle pulled up out back. A minute later, the door swung open, and this time, Todd Burk walked through. As he did, the others rose to their feet, as though they'd been waiting on him to do something.

Her blood turned to ice.

She wasn't the only one who had picked up on the ominous vibe. The few remaining customers threw money on the tables for their bills and skedaddled out the front door.

"This feels like something else." Xavier kept his voice low. "Something bigger. What did you do?"

"Asked questions."

"About them?" His eyebrows shot up. "At Custom Gears? You left out the part about your sudden interest in motorcycles being related to them."

The devil was in the details, but she hadn't realized when she'd gone there that she would bring trouble to Delgado's. Or to herself, for that matter.

Maybe this was a good sign. Good being relative. They were approaching her in a public place, which was reason to give her hope that this scenario would not end in a horrific, painful and possibly deadly way.

Right?

Now, if they had been waiting for her in the dark, inside her cottage, then that would be a much different story. One where the odds would not look good that she would be walking away from the confrontation.

Her cell phone vibrated. Quickly, she answered without looking at who it was. "Yes."

"Hey, it's me," Holden said over the other end. "Rodney admitted to the harassment and the snakes." The sound of his voice soothed her and heightened her worries at the same time.

She didn't want him walking into the middle of whatever was about to happen here. Something told her that these men didn't abide by the law, didn't respect authority and would use any opportunity to physically hurt Holden if they could.

"I'll need you to file charges against him," he said. "But Rodney didn't try to run you off the road. And he didn't slash your tires."

Half-focused on what he was saying, Grace clenched and unclenched her other hand nervously at her side. She'd thought for certain that Rodney had been behind all of that and once Holden had him in jail, she wouldn't have to worry about it anymore. "Are you sure?"

"He has no reason to confess to the other things and deny the rest," Holden said. "It wouldn't make any sense. I think someone else is responsible for those things."

Bad news she didn't need, but she would have to contend with it later. Right now she had a more pressing matter.

Todd strode up to the bar, staring straight at her.

"I have to go," she said, keeping her tone low and matter-of-fact.

"What's wrong?" Holden asked. "I can hear it in your voice."

Something was developing. Something ugly. She wanted to tell him, but she had created this mess and needed to deal with it on her own.

"There's an urgent customer service problem," she said. "I have to call you back."

"Grace," Holden said, his voice tightening.

She disconnected before he could finish that statement.

This situation—whatever it was—was more pressing.

Todd dropped down on one of the barstools in front of her while the rest of his guys remained standing. "You." He pointed to Xavier but kept staring at her. "Get me a shot of bourbon."

Xavier looked to her. Without taking her eyes off Todd, she nodded for him to do it.

That particular Iron Warrior had taken dramatic measures to command her full attention and she was going to give it to him.

Xavier hurried and put a glass down. With a shaking hand, he poured the liquor in, splashing some on the bar. "That's on the house."

Her throat tightened like she was choking. She was so baffled and scared. This was of a different magnitude than Rodney popping up, or the snakes.

Somehow this was much, much worse.

Todd threw the shot back in one gulp. Turning over the glass, he set it on the bar with a clink. His gaze never left her the entire time, burning a hole through her. "You. Will. Stop."

She swallowed past the lump in her throat. "Stop what?" she croaked.

"Sniffing around where your nose doesn't belong," Todd said, conversationally.

"I think there's a misunderstanding," Grace said, needing to the defuse the volatile situation before things escalated.

Todd shook his head. "No misunderstanding on my part." He lifted a finger and wagged it up and down in her direction and said, "But there is on yours."

She kept her sights zeroed in on him and did it awhile until it hit her that his comment begged a question that he was waiting for her to ask. "About what?"

"Thursday night." He tossed the words out and they hung in the air worse than a foul odor. "You didn't see anything. You certainly didn't hear anything, like a Milwaukee-Eight big twin engine. Did you?"

More ice slinked over her skin.

It was too late. She'd already spoken to Holden about everything she knew. The man fighting with Emma. The black motorcycle.

A Harley.

A model that Todd rode.

"What if I did?" she asked, the question flying out of her mouth in a knee-jerk reaction, before she had a chance to think and consider the consequences.

Xavier gasped and backed away, putting plenty of room between himself and her.

She cringed on the inside, wanting to haul the words back into her mouth. But since they were out there, she straightened and crossed her arms to hide the trembling of her hands.

Todd's expression remained deadpan as he tipped his head to the side toward a big fellow.

That was when the burly guy, who was standing beside him, drew the biggest knife Grace had ever seen. He thrust the blade into the bar, driving it deep into the mahogany wood.

The action, *the sound* of it plunging in, sent her staggering backward with a flinch.

"Curiosity killed the cat," the man growled, leaning forward, glaring at her.

Oh, God.

That was not a hollow promise. That was a threat.

A cold sweat broke out on her back and ran down her spine. She'd been scared, but now she was terrified. These men were ruthless and could easily follow through. They could get to her at any time out on Old Mill Road, with no one around to hear her scream.

Had they followed her last night? Run her off the road as a prelude to this?

"Did one of you…" She cleared her throat when the words came out choked. "Did one of you try to run me off the road last night?"

"If we come for someone, we make sure they know it's us," Todd said, easily. "Otherwise, it would defeat the purpose."

She looked at all the Iron Warriors crowding the bar, making their presence unmistakably felt, bearing down heavier than sandbags on her chest, squeezing the air from her lungs.

"Did you see us last night?" Todd asked, motioning to the men gathered around him. "See any of our cuts?" He gestured to his motorcycle vest that was prominently on display. "Hear any of our bikes?"

It had been someone in a truck, blinding her with high beams. She had no idea who had been driving, but there hadn't been any motorcycles on the road.

She shook her head. "No." Even if she had seen them, she was ready to stick with that answer. *See no evil. Hear no evil. Etcetera.*

"I've only got one more thing to say to you," he said, "in case it hasn't sunken in."

She prayed that meant he and the rest of the tough-looking guys in his club would leave soon. So she quickly asked, "What?"

Gaze still glued to her, Todd rose slowly from his seat, scraping the stool back against the hardwood floor.

She braced, not knowing what was going to happen, but in doing it, she feared her body would splinter to pieces. Still, she kept her attention keen on him. The terrible sensation of her insides twisting went on far too long as he just stood there, staring at her, sucking up all the oxygen from the room.

When she thought she'd beg for him to spit it out, he uttered a single word.

"Stop."

She heard the menace.

Hell, she felt it, too, since it was clogging the room.

Then Todd gave her a strange, frightening smile that sent a chill down her spine. He looked to the men in the room, jerked his head toward the door and walked out.

The guy with the knife yanked it out of the wood, shoved it into a holster on his hip and followed him along with the others, each one of them scowling at her on their way out.

Once they had all gone outside, she let out the breath she had been holding. Her legs trembled as though they might give out. She bent over and clutched her thighs, and now her breaths came in rasps.

Xavier swore. "That was a message. They were sending you a message!"

People left voice mails, sent texts, used email, even telegrams to send a message.

No, this had been far worse. They had given her a warning. "Yeah, I got that."

"Whatever you've been doing, you better stop." Xavier sounded terrified like he had been the one threatened. He ran his fingers over the thick gash in the mahogany wood. "They stabbed the bar with a freaking bowie knife," he said, and she thought it was good to know what it was called. "Hunters use those to butcher and skin prey."

Fitting weapon for that pack of predators.

"Unless you have a death wish," he said, "you need to stop."

Motorcycles fired up outside, the engines creating a deafening roar that echoed their threat. They stayed out back, revving their Harleys for what seemed like forever, though it was only a few minutes. The sound washed over her, through her, reverberating in the marrow of her bones.

They finally pulled away from Delgado's. But the

ferocious growl and the intense, menacing vibration of their bikes stayed with her. Along with the terror they had stoked.

Chapter Twelve

The powerful rumble of motorcycles, the exhaust-crackling bellow gripped Holden before he caught sight of them. There were at least twenty. They rounded the corner, hitting Third Street.

Had they come from Delgado's? Had the Iron Warriors been there? Had they gone to intimidate Grace?

Was that why she'd hung up on him?

The group of motorcycles rode slowly in formation. In no apparent hurry, as though parading through town, deliberately making a spectacle. They wanted their presence known—seen, felt and heard.

Their growling engines ran riot over Holden's nerves.

Out front, leading the pack, wasn't Rip. It was Todd Burk. Their gazes collided as they passed each other.

The skin on the back of Holden's neck prickled, and it was as if someone had just walked over his grave.

But his only thought was of Grace.

The Iron Warriors hit their throttles and zoomed off.

Holden did likewise, pressing down on the gas, going over the speed the limit. Just beating the light before it flashed from yellow to red, he took a sharp left turn, zipping around the corner. He cut into the parking lot behind Delgado's and parked. Hurried from the vehicle. Rushed through the door.

Not a single customer was inside. The place was quiet and empty. Except for Grace and Xavier, who both sat at the bar. *Drinking.*

She was a self-admitted lightweight when it came to alcohol and never drank in the middle of the day, much less on the job.

That was enough to confirm to him that the Iron Warriors had in fact been there.

"What did they want?" Holden asked, marching up to her.

Xavier poured her another shot of whiskey.

She swallowed with a grimace and coughed. "To give me a warning."

"About?" he asked, coming up alongside her, and put a hand on her back.

"Getting involved."

Xavier shook his head, pouring himself another drink. "About sticking her nose where it didn't belong. She needs to stay out of it. Keep quiet. Say she didn't see anything. Hear anything. Specifically, a particular type of V-twin engine."

Grace sighed. "I've gotten myself in a jam." She looked up at him, her eyes clouded and sad and full of fear. "I don't know how to get out of it."

But he knew how to get her out.

The Powell name, all his family's money and power, as mighty as it was, wouldn't be able to put a stop to the Iron Warriors and Todd.

Only one thing could.

The law.

Holden rubbed her back to reassure her it would be okay. He'd find a way. Somehow.

She turned to him, wrapping her arms around him in a hug. He pulled her up to her feet and tightened the embrace. Held her with his chin on the top of her head, giving her comfort, for as long as she needed.

After a few moments, she pulled back and put one hand on the bar and the other on her hip. "I'm in over my head. Maybe I should go to California for a few days, spend the holidays with my mom, until this is resolved."

His heart clenched.

He'd already envisioned spending Christmas Eve with her, surrounded by his family, who'd make her feel welcome and put her at ease. They'd get to know her better, firsthand, see why he was so drawn to her. So captivated.

She'd be safe. Let her guard down. Have fun, without worry of judgment.

All the things she deserved.

But it was more than that. This didn't sound like her. Grace didn't surrender. She dug in and fought, even if it looked like a losing battle.

"Where is this coming from?" Holden asked. She didn't want to abandon the cottage. She didn't want to leave Wyoming. "Is that really what you want? To be with Selene?"

Grace rolled her eyes and lowered her head.

"Leaving for a few days would be for the best," Xavier said. "The Iron Warriors meant business." He took another shot of whiskey. "They scared *me* sense-less. I thought I'd have a heart attack, and I had nothing to do with it."

This was Xavier's bright idea—for her to flee town and head back to California, where she didn't belong.

"Maybe he's right," Grace said, sounding defeated. "My mom already offered to buy me a ticket. All I have to do is call her. No groveling necessary. She could probably book me on a nonstop flight out of Denver tonight."

"They've got one leaving at eight," Xavier said, looking at flights on his phone. "It's only a two-and-a-half-hour flight nonstop. You should call your mother right now. There are only three tickets left."

Holden groaned, wanting Xavier to shut up. The man meant well, but he wasn't helping.

Grace had never been straightforward with Holden about her relationship with her mother. Her responses were always cagey, but he had read between the lines. Taken in her body language, heard the things she didn't say.

He knew.

To call their relationship strained would be putting it mildly. Selene, the glamourous, bewitching, one-time supermodel made Grace feel inadequate, as though she would never be enough for her mother, and still wanted her daughter to run on a hamster wheel in search of her approval, which would always be just out of reach.

Grace would go to California for the holidays, where she would be miserable, over his dead body.

"Running away isn't the answer," Holden said. "You're not leaving."

A small smile tugged at her lips but worry swam in her eyes. Her face turned haggard with fear.

Xavier jumped to his feet. "You don't know what it was like with them here. They stabbed the bar with a damn bowie knife." He pointed to a gouge in the wood of the bar. "They'll skin her alive if she's the reason Todd Burk goes down."

Then she wouldn't be.

"Be quiet," Holden snapped at Xavier. The man rocked back on his heels and sat down. Cutting his gaze from him, Holden looked at Grace and clutched her shoulders. "I can fix this. I can get Todd and keep you safe."

"How? I don't want you to put yourself in harm's way. You can't threaten or intimidate them. They're not Rodney."

Didn't he know it.

"Putting myself in harm's way comes with the job." But he would walk through fire to protect Grace. When she grimaced, he gave her a hopeful smile. "But that's not part of my plan. Do you trust me?"

"With my life," she said without hesitation.

That was all he needed to hear. "Then you're staying here. And I'm going to go fix it. Right now."

She pressed a palm to his cheek. "How? I need to know you'll be okay."

"By taking the attention off you. You can't identify who killed Emma or the bike he was riding. Those are facts. Testimony from you wouldn't put anyone away." He'd make it so that she never even had to enter a courtroom. "I'm going to do my job, follow procedure, follow the trail until I have the cold, hard evidence we need." He was going to start by following his gut instincts.

"Promise me you'll be careful," she said, letting her hand fall from his face.

"I will. Don't worry."

"I don't know how not to."

"Start by playing some Christmas music in here and then think about how you're *not* going to spend the holidays locked up in a Pacific Palisades prison with the Grinch."

Grace smiled and the sight of her smile lit up his world. It was all he needed.

Twenty minutes later, Holden found himself on the opposite end of Third Street, stalking into the Fierce & Sassy nail salon.

Nikki looked up at him from behind the reception desk. She tensed, her eyes going wide. Her mouth opened. "You can't be in here." She glanced around at the customers noticing his presence, which only seemed to amplify her alarm.

"Actually, I can." Resting a forearm on the counter, he leaned toward her. "Plan on staying, too. For as long as necessary."

"No, no, no," she said in a harsh, low voice, her eyes narrowing. "You have to leave." Nikki was the type of woman who slapped on too much makeup that made her look older than she was, with signature cherry-red lipstick and nails like long talons. She always wore revealing clothing. Low-cut tops revealing plenty of cleavage. Short-short skirts that ended midthigh and sky-high heels, regardless of the weather.

She dressed like a gangster's girlfriend was expected to.

"It's been slow around the office with it being the holidays. I'm free to stay." He raised his voice a bit. "All day."

"I've got nothing to say to you. Not now. Not ever. Now get gone." Then she mouthed, *"Please, I'll do anything."*

That was the nature of the rapport they'd built over the past couple of years. For the sake of appearances, she talked a good game, did a lot blustering and pretended to stand her ground. But he'd learned that if he got her alone, with no prying eyes to report back to Todd, she opened up to him. She had confided in him on a number of occasions about her boyfriend's abuse, although she wouldn't press charges.

She'd also shared that there were issues in the MC dividing the members. Some, like Rip, wanted the club to take the straight and narrow path of only engaging in legal pursuits. The others enjoyed the money and perks of their illicit activities.

Based on the group following Todd earlier, it looked like he was winning the battle.

Holden slipped the note from his clenched hand and let it fall to the other side of the desk in front of her. Meeting her eyes, he tipped his hat and left.

From the sidewalk he looked back at her. Head bent, she was reading the note he'd written.

*Meet me at Divine Treats in three hours. They'll
be closed for the day. We'll talk there. Privately.
Discreetly. Or I come back to Fierce & Sassy.
I'll be loud and it'll be ugly.*

Raising her head, Nikki gave a furtive glance around.
Then she looked at Holden and nodded.

THE DOOR WAS UNLOCKED when Nikki strode inside. Her
three-inch heels click-clacking across the tile floor.

Holden was waiting behind the counter. "Turn the
bolt and follow me." He didn't want anyone wandering
in by mistake, thinking the pastry shop was open. Most
folks knew the bakery closed at four in the afternoon,
but he wasn't taking any chances.

Nikki did as he told her.

Amy and the others had cleared out and agreed to
come back later to finish cleaning up.

"What do you want?" Nikki spat out, flouncing into
the kitchen, where no one would be able to see them
from the street.

"I want the truth. You and Todd are lying. He wasn't
with you at the clubhouse on Thursday."

Nikki put a hand on her hip. "Says who?"

"Says common sense. The good Lord gave me some.
A bunch of strippers were at the clubhouse that night."
There was no way that Todd was there with Nikki,
watching the show or doing things with the entertain-
ment that would've made his girlfriend extremely angry
if she had been present. "So I know you weren't there."

"That's supposition. Not proof."

"One of these days, Todd is going to knock all your teeth out. Rupture a spleen. Give you brain damage. Or simply kill you. It's possible he might do all of the above. Wouldn't you like to see him pay for some other crime before then?"

Nikki moistened her lips, probably salivating at the thought of seeing him pay for something other than killing her.

She crossed her arms and leaned against one of the large commercial ovens. "How do I know that whatever I say to you won't get traced back to me? Because if he knows I talked to you, he will kill me and find a way to get away with it. He gets away with everything."

Holden's job was to protect and serve. Especially those who wouldn't or couldn't protect themselves. He wouldn't do anything to bring Todd's wrath down on her head.

"When he kicked you out of the club," he said, "or you stormed off irate, I'm sure you didn't go home to sulk while he was out having a good time. Did you?"

She shrugged. "Let's say it went down that way and I didn't go home. Then what?"

He was on the right track. "Then you probably went out with your girls," he said, and her eyes brightened. "Had some fun without any men. All I need is one credit charge you made somewhere that night. A traffic camera you passed that says you were somewhere else. I can pull all that without anybody talking to me."

She hesitated, thinking about it, weighing her options. Probably comparing how much she loved Todd versus how much she hated him. "I went to the Wild Pony that night with my girls. Like you thought."

The saloon/dance hall was located over in Cheyenne, about an hour's drive. They had live country music, line dancing, a mechanical bull. The works for a good time.

"Did you use your credit card?" he asked.

She nodded. "Yeah. I bought a few rounds of drinks. One close to midnight, for sure."

"Thank you."

"His alibi with me may be garbage. But I think he lied about being with me, in front of all of his brothers, to protect me."

"From what?"

"The humiliation of everyone knowing that he was really with another woman that night." She chewed on her lip and stared at her feet. "I think he was with some stripper. Probably Misty. He's got a thing for her."

Holden stared at her with pity. Todd cheated on her, beat her, disrespected her, and not only did she stay with him and defend him, but she also honestly believed that his lie had been to protect her.

"You know, Nikki, it's possible he could've killed Emma and then gone back to the club and slept with a stripper. Maybe he lied to protect himself." Because he didn't have an alibi.

A couple of tears leaked from her eyes and rolled down her cheek. "I don't want to believe he would do that. Hurt Emma. Because if he killed her, then he might really be capable of killing me, too, one day." She squeezed her eyes shut. "I don't... I can't..."

There was a *but* that wanted to come. A big one. He heard it. Sensed it. Felt it deep in his bones. "But what?"

Nikki looked up at him, smudged mascara giving her raccoon eyes, her cherry-red lips trembling. "I found something on his bedside table at the clubhouse. It hadn't been there before. I didn't understand why he had it, or where he got it from. And when I asked him about it, he got so angry with me. I'm talking furious. He grabbed me by my face and told me that I hadn't seen it. Never to say a word about it."

Holden stepped forward, getting closer. This was it. A vital piece to the puzzle he needed. "What did you see?"

She sniffled and wiped tears from her eyes. "Do you promise you can put him away?"

The Iron Warriors had given the man the fitting nickname *Teflon*. Because charges never stuck to him.

"I promise I will do my absolute best," Holden said. "Trust me, I want him behind bars more than most." They had a history and Todd had a lot to pay for. "What did you find?"

"A Shining Light necklace."

Emma's.

The one that had been missing when Holden had found her.

Chapter Thirteen

Dread that had filled Grace since Todd's visit washed over her again, drenching her like a sudden downpour. She couldn't stop worrying about Holden and whether he was endangering himself to fix a problem she had created.

Although this was a small town, where almost everyone knew everyone, it had never occurred to her that someone might report back to Todd. In her wildest dreams she could not have imagined that they would show up in full force to coerce one woman into silence.

So, if all that had been beyond the scope of her imagination, there was no telling what they might do to Holden.

She admired his strength and his optimism. He was fearless. She just didn't want him paying the price for her mistake.

"Why don't you go home and lie low?" Xavier suggested, looking at the handful of customers that had trickled in during what would normally be a bustling dinner rush. "At least until lover boy comes up with a solution."

"Lover boy?" she asked, not liking the insulting and inaccurate sound of it. "What do you mean?"

"You and Holden." He waited. When she didn't respond, he went on, "It's obvious you two are dating."

"But we're not."

"Then why is he in here all the time?"

"He's single and doesn't like to cook. He comes in here all the time with Nash and Mitch."

Xavier scoffed. "Oh, please. He comes in twice a day since you started working here. Once with them for dinner and once in the afternoon on his own to have pie. Why doesn't he simply have his pie after supper? Instead, he also buys you a slice, eating it across the table from you, chatting and looking at you like he wants to spoon you up, too."

"He wasn't coming in for pie before I took over as manager?" She had thought it was just his routine. Some people were creatures of habit, and she wasn't one to judge.

"Are you kidding me?" A scathing laugh rolled from him. "I'm surprised he can still squeeze into his uniform. Before you, he was in here maybe a couple of times a week. Not a couple of times a day. And how about the way he showed up here this afternoon like a white knight with a shining badge to rescue you."

She opened her mouth to throw out a quip about how she didn't need rescuing, but lately that wasn't true. She had needed Holden's help with the snakes, and once again, she needed assistance extricating herself from a dangerous situation with the Iron Warriors.

Grace was no damsel, but she was in distress.

"Maybe I can go back to Custom Gears. Talk to Kyle. Tell him I'll keep quiet and won't say anything. Ask him to relay the message to his brother." But she reminded herself that she had already said plenty to the authorities, which couldn't be taken back.

"Don't make things worse," Xavier said. "Just go home. Drown your sorrows." He handed her the bottle of whiskey. "It's on me. I'll close tonight."

Every time she'd tried to help, she'd miscalculated and had gotten herself into trouble.

Xavier was only looking out for her. If she wasn't going to take his advice to leave town—an idea she abhorred— she might as well go home early tonight. Have a drink or two and see if she could manage sleeping in her own bed, alone, without imagining snakes.

HOLDEN FINISHED EXPLAINING the situation of how Todd Burk had lied about his alibi, thus giving the sheriff's office justification to get a warrant. Not only to search his premises, but also to get forensics on his motorcycle.

Now he waited on the phone to hear the verdict.

Once the Honorable Judge Don Rumpke was finished hemming and hawing, he said, "You have evidence that he lied, not just the word of his girlfriend, who might be feeling a little vindictive?"

This judge wasn't in the pocket of the Iron Warriors and despised what the MC had become under the influence of Todd Burk. In the scandal that had ruined Holden's reputation, the judge had not doubted Holden's innocence, but he did believe that the sheriff's office would have been better off firing him and starting with a clean slate.

And instead of whispering behind his back, Judge Rumpke had been quite vocal about his perspective, to Holden's face. Holden and the judge might not get along, but Holden trusted the man.

"Yes," Holden said. "I ran her credit card history and spoke with a bartender at the Wild Pony. She was there the evening in question. From nine p.m. to one in the morning."

"All right, then. You can have your warrant," Rumpke said, and Holden hit the air with his fist in celebration. "Tomorrow."

It was always *tomorrow* with this guy. Holden stifled a groan. "Your Honor—"

"Save your breath, Holden. It's seven thirty at night. On a Saturday. My wife and I are in Cheyenne. We just finished Christmas shopping for our grandkids. Now, I'm about to take her to have a nice dinner. We are in the restaurant's parking lot as I speak."

"I can send you the paperwork electronically for an e-signature."

"Are you listening? I'm not working right now. Besides, I don't have a smartphone. We're spending the night at her sister's here in Cheyenne. I'll be back tomorrow and will do you the favor of taking care of it on a Sunday afternoon, the Lord's Day when I should be resting, and on Christmas Eve no less, to issue you the warrant. Unless you have reason to believe that Mr. Burk will abscond between now and then. Do you?"

Holden pounded his fist against the desk in frustration. "No, Your Honor. I do not."

"Well, all right, then."

"Can we make it the morning, sir?"

"Are you living at the sheriff's office these days? Doesn't your shift start around noon?"

"I would come in early for this, sir."

"Don't bother. Get your rest, son. The missus and I have church service in the morning with her sister. I'll be in after. Good night." Rumpke hung up.

Holden gritted his teeth as he set down the landline in his office.

There was no time to stew over how he was going to have to wait until tomorrow to slap handcuffs on Todd, because Ashley was waving him over through the glass window, which overlooked the deputies' desks.

He hurried over to see what she and Mitch had discovered. "What did you find?"

Ashley hopped out of her chair and motioned for him to sit. "You were right. She walked to the Dogbane Express. A little service station a mile and a half from Jared's place. It has the closest pay phone. She used it. The station manager gave us copies of both of his surveillance feeds from the night. In and outside the store."

With a couple of clicks on her keyboard, she brought up the footage.

Emma Burk appeared on the screen, walking through the front door of the store. Shivering, she rubbed her hands together and blew on them. She spoke to the attendant, who pointed to the back of the store. Nodding, Emma headed that way. She got on the pay phone.

"It looks like she made a collect call," Ashley said. "I rewound it numerous times, slowed it down. She never went in her pockets, and it doesn't look like she deposited any money."

"We can request the records," Mitch said. "See whom she called."

Holden nodded, but not with enthusiasm. "The telephone companies are notoriously slow to respond to a warrant. It can take weeks. Sometimes longer to get the records we've requested. Once we waited two months."

Mitch gave a low whistle. "Sheesh. That is a long time."

"There's more," Ashley said, fast-forwarding. "Emma waited inside the store fifteen minutes. Then her ride shows up." She toggled some keys, bringing up the video feed from the surveillance camera outside the store.

Come on. Show us his face. Or the license plate. Anything.

"The bike pulls up just out of view," Ashley said. "All we can see are the tires and him putting his foot down as he steadies the bike and waits for her." She pointed to the far part of the screen.

The guy wore black steel-toed riding boots. Just like everyone else on a motorcycle. Emma walked over and then climbed on.

"Wait a minute," Holden said. "Rewind it to where Emma leaves the store." Ashley went back to where he indicated. "Right there. Look. See how she hesitates. Whoever it is that shows up has to wait on her. She goes outside, stands there, like she's not sure."

"Second-guessing whether he was the right person to call," Ashley said.

"Clearly he wasn't," Mitch chimed in.

"But she gets on the bike anyway." Holden stared at the screen. "Why would she?"

"Maybe she was desperate," Ashley said. "Tired and cold and just wanted to go back to the B and B to get some sleep."

"But why not simply call someone from the Shining Light to pick her up?" Mitch asked. "She was going back tomorrow anyway. Why bother spending her last night at the B and B? Why risk calling someone she didn't trust?"

That was the million-dollar question.

The only problem was Emma no longer trusted anyone on the outside. Only the people in the Shining Light compound.

"Are there any traffic cameras between the Iron Warriors clubhouse and the Dogbane Express?" Holden asked.

"Afraid not." Mitch shook his head. "We thought to check."

"What about from the service station to the B and B? They might've been caught on camera, and we'd have a license plate."

Ashley frowned. "We tried that, too. But the driver was careful. He deliberately took the back roads. Stayed away from any main intersections."

"That's typical Iron Warriors MO," Holden said, and Ashley nodded.

They wanted anyone who was a target of their hostility to know it was them, but they always did a great job covering their tracks.

It was time for the tides to turn and for the scales to be balanced. Come tomorrow, he would have his warrant, and justice would be served.

THE SOUND OF the wind tugged Grace from a deep sleep. Instead of a drawn-out howl, it crackled and sputtered and roared.

She was so tired, and her limbs were heavy. All she wanted to do was to rest a little longer.

But that sound.

As her eyelids lifted, she immediately sensed something was wrong. But her thoughts were sluggish and scattered. Probably from the whiskey. Her body was slow to move. Also from the booze. Then the smell hit her.

Smoke.

Where was it coming from?

She climbed out of the bed wearing her nightgown and socks, and went toward the bedroom door.

An orange glow illuminated the smoke wafting into the room from under the door. She clutched the doorknob, but it wasn't cool metal that greeted her palm. The knob was warm to the touch.

Grace opened the door.

Flames were everywhere, dancing and devouring the cabin all along the perimeter. Fire licked up the walls, over the log structure, rippling across the ceiling. Smoke pinched her lungs, causing her to cough. Every breath she took hurt.

She covered her mouth and nose with her hand. Shock pulsed through her.

Part of her wanted to believe this wasn't really happening—just a terrible, horrible nightmare, and if she woke up, she would be safe.

But this was real. And it would kill her.

Burning chunks of wood—pieces of the cabin—fell to smolder in the fire tearing through the cottage. It had already swept across the living room, raging closer.

She had to get out.

Her gaze darted to the door with watering eyes. The room was too bright and too hazy with smoke at the same time, making it hard to see. But the blaze had consumed the front door. She whirled toward the back one by the kitchen. The exit was only a few feet away, but it was useless to her. The door was engulfed in flames. Even the curtains over the windows in the living and dining rooms had caught fire, trapping her in the burning cabin.

Fear mingled with the smoke, clogging her lungs, making it harder to breathe. Her eyes stung and watered, blurring her vision of the flames and smoke.

Waves of immense, suffocating heat bore down on her. The flames pressed in, eating up the oxygen.

Staggering back into the bedroom, she slammed the door closed.

Think.

What to do?

Coughing, she rushed to the bureau and, dropping to her knees, opened the bottom drawer. She grabbed some towels and stuffed them under the door to keep out as much of the smoke as possible.

But that wouldn't stop the fire. She had to find another way out. Forcing her thoughts to clear and focus, she looked around.

The window by the bed. She ran to it and threw back the curtains. Throwing back the top latch to unlock it, she shoved upward. But the window didn't budge. Again she tried, pushing it with all the force she could muster.

She snatched the pointed nail file from her nightstand. Using the pointed tip, she scraped at the paint along the seams. That was when she saw it.

The window had been nailed shut.

No, no, no!

Heart pounding against her rib cage, she struggled to think. Only one thing was clear. If she didn't do something, she was going to die. She needed to hurry.

Break it.

Break the glass!

She glanced around in a panic, searching to find something—*anything*—to use. Her gaze landed on the tall floor lamp in the corner of the room. The base of it was wide and thick and heavy. It would work well to bust the window.

Yanking the cord from the socket, she grabbed and hoisted it up.

A crunching sound thundered overhead as the cabin trembled around her, snapping her to a halt. With a booming crack, part of the ceiling caved in. A large beam dropped, crashing onto the bed, spewing a flurry of angry sparks throughout the room. The blazing beam glowed red as though it had been spat from the mouth of hell and now blocked the window.

Her one chance. Her last way to escape was gone.

The cabin was on fire, being reduced to ash around her, and she was trapped inside.

Oh, God. Please.

I don't want to die. Not like this! Burned alive.

Her mind screamed at her to move. To run from the vicious heat of the blinding flames and the oppressive smoke.

Dizziness swamped her. Each breath was poison. If the fire didn't kill her, the smoke surely would.

Hacking on the smoke, her eyes stinging, she grabbed a blanket from the bureau and her cell phone from the top of it. She rushed to get away from the fire and ducked into the bathroom.

There were no windows in there. No possible way out.

Tears leaked from her eyes. This time not from the smoke. But she was not going to simply give up and die, sobbing and blubbering.

She was going to fight. Even if it was with her last breath, she would fight to survive.

Shaking, she tossed the blanket into the bathtub and turned on the faucet. Grabbing the towel hanging on the back of the door, she stuffed it underneath to plug the space. Once the blanket was thoroughly soaked, she shut off the faucet.

Then she did the only thing left that she could do.

She climbed into the tub under the wet bedspread and dialed 911.

Chapter Fourteen

At Delgado's, Holden had been disappointed and relieved to find that Grace had gone home early. It was about time that Xavier stopped taking advantage of her kindness and started closing more often.

He was headed to her place to let her know face-to-face that Todd would be in custody tomorrow without it tying back to her. Any evidence collected would not be associated with her and the attention would be elsewhere.

Namely on him and the sheriff's department. They had a job to do and the investigation steered them to Todd. He was the one who had lied about his alibi and got caught, resulting in the warrant. In the search, he'd find Emma's missing necklace and the forensics from his bike would match the paint that had transferred to the rented vehicle. None of which would have anything to do with Grace.

Getting her involved beyond taking her statement had been his mistake. Now he'd rectify it.

As he turned on to Old Mill, the smoke caught his attention first. There was a lot of it.

Coming from Grace's place.

He sped down the gravel road, his back tires spitting loose rocks as he swerved, the truck threatening to fishtail. Through the trees lining the road, he caught sight of the flames. *Dear God.* The whole cottage was on fire.

A call came through on his cell. It was the station. He stabbed the answer icon on the screen. "Listen to me. There's a fire at Grace's place."

"We know." Ashley's voice was grave. "First two emergency calls that came in only gave the address. We didn't realize the house was hers. Then Grace just phoned in. She's trapped inside," she said, sending his adrenaline into overdrive. "In the bathroom. The fire department is already on the way."

Grace was trapped. But she was alive. For now.

He yanked the wheel, whipping into Grace's driveway, and the cottage came into full view. A brilliant orange-and-yellow blaze lit up the black night. Nearly the entire house was engulfed in flames, including the roof.

Even Grace's car was on fire.

His heart stuttered at the sight. The fire department wouldn't reach her in time.

In front of the house, he slammed on the brakes, threw the truck in Park and jumped out. He opened his back door, dug into garment bag and fished out his old T-shirt. Reaching up front, he grabbed a bottle of water from the cup holder.

He hopped out, moving toward the burning cottage while he soaked the T-shirt with the water.

Choking smoke and unbearable heat radiated from the inferno. The roar of the fire was deafening. Climbing the porch steps, he covered his nose and mouth with the T-shirt. Glass suddenly broke, spraying outward as the windows burst and molten gold flames lashed out.

His feet faltered to a halt. But only for a moment. He kicked open the front door.

Crackling, wild flames clawed out to meet him. Searing heat licked his skin. His lungs burned. Still, he rushed inside to get to Grace.

A raging fire had swallowed the living room. Flames danced up the walls, across the floor and furniture. Fiery chunks of the ceiling crumbled in front of him, raining scorching sparks in his one path. And the insufferable heat was hot as hellfire, pushing him back outside.

He stumbled onto the porch, patting his sleeves where sparks and embers had landed, igniting his jacket.

There was no way through. He wasn't wearing the proper clothing and shoes for the job, but he had to reach her somehow.

He screamed on the inside with no choice but to backtrack off the porch. Keying his radio, he contacted the station. "How long until the fire department gets here?" he yelled over the crackling howl of the fire.

"Seven minutes."

Grace was running out of time. Once the roof timbers burned through, the entire ceiling was going to collapse and that would be the end. The roof was already on fire and could go at any second. She didn't have that long to wait; she needed help, right this second.

Panic skittered up his spine, threatening to consume him, but he persevered.

The bathroom.

She's in the bathroom.

Remembering what Ashley had told him, he took off for the right side of the house. He snatched the ax from the tree stump that she used to chop wood and bolted to his truck. It was still running. Throwing it in gear, he sped around to the other side where the bathroom was located and pulled up in front of it.

There were no windows. But there was a vent. It was only six inches in width and length, but it was the best place to start.

He hopped out and climbed up on top of the truck's hood. That gave him the extra height he needed to reach the bathroom vent that was connected to the exterior wall.

Not wasting any precious time, he swung the ax, smashing into the vent. *Hurry, hurry, hurry.* A few good whacks and he had ripped clean through it, tearing the entire unit out.

"Grace!" He looked through the opening. It wasn't quite big enough for her to fit through, yet, but he could see her.

She peered up at him from the tub from beneath a wet blanket. "Holden!" She climbed out.

"Stand back," he warned, not wanting bits of flying debris to cut her.

Sirens were in the distance. Still a few miles away. They would be there soon.

But he would have her out by then.

He swung the ax with all his might, again and again, chopping away at the wall, making the opening larger.

His hands were slippery with sweat and fear, his heart hammering in his chest. Each devastating swing brought him closer to her. He slashed at the wood in a frenzy. Faster and faster. Not slowing to catch his breath. With only one thought pounding through his brain.

Save Grace. Get her out.

If necessary, he'd tear down the wall with his bare hands. One way or another, he would get to her.

Once the hole was big enough, he reached through. "Come on!"

She dropped the bedspread and rushed over to the toilet. Thankfully, she was wearing socks, which would somewhat protect her feet from sharp debris. Standing on top of the toilet, she took his hands and he hoisted her up until he could get a hold of her under her arms. With a firm grasp, he pulled her through the hole in the wall.

He lowered her to the hood and brought her against his chest and wrapped his arms around her. He was finally able to breathe, just like Grace. Her body went limp against him, but her arms tightened around him. Caressing her hair, he held her close and would for as long as she allowed.

Even outside in the fresh air on this side of the house, the smoke was overwhelming. The wind didn't carry it away so much as whipping the smoke up, making it hard to breathe standing so close to the fire.

Reluctantly, he let her go. Then he took off his jacket and put it around her. "We've got to get back from the house." He jumped down from the hood and held up his arms to her.

He helped her climb down, but before her socked

feet touched the cold, hard ground, he lifted her into his arms. Hurrying around to the side of the truck, where his door was wide-open, he set her down on the driver's seat. She shimmied over the console to the passenger's side, making room for him.

Throwing the truck in Reverse, he sped back away from the house and into the driveway. Just as they reached it, giving them both a view of the entire house, the burning roof collapsed with a nerve-wracking crash.

Thank God he'd gotten her out in time.

Grace could've still been inside. The firefighters inbound could have as well, creating a life-and-death situation for all of them.

What would have happened to her if he hadn't already been on the way to see her?

He glanced over, meeting her eyes.

"You came. If you hadn't…" A single tear escaped and rolled down her cheek. "You got me out in time."

"I would do anything for you." It was true. He hadn't realized it until now, but he would take on any pain, any burden for her.

Her smile was breathtaking as she reached for him, and he leaned over, pulling her to him.

"I almost lost you," he whispered. The words, their meaning, resonated through him, scaring him in a different way. But being this close to her, his head spinning and his heart racing too fast, he dismissed it as residual adrenaline from the fear of coming so close to danger and within a hair's breadth of having her snatched from his life. "Do you know how the fire started?"

She shook her head. "I dozed off. When I woke up, the cottage was burning down around me."

He held her closer, tighter. Smoke inhalation was deadly. It was the number one cause of death related to fires. Without an alarm, most people never woke up when smoke filled a house. It numbed the senses, causing deeper sleep. If she hadn't awakened…

He shuddered to think of it.

"The smoke detector never went off?" he asked, pulling back to look at her.

"No. I don't know why. I had one installed after I moved in." She coughed with a wince. "And I tried to open the bedroom window to get out through there, but it had been nailed shut."

"What?" Someone had deliberately tried to trap her in the house and set it on fire?

"Did you release Rodney?"

"No. He's still sitting in a cell." Writing her an apology letter. "It couldn't have been him."

But someone had done this. Perhaps the same person who had run her off the road and slashed her tires.

Sirens blared, red and white strobes flashed, as the fire engine, with the welcome scream of its horn, and an EMS vehicle pulled up past them, stopping near the house.

Firefighters raced to grab the hose, though the cabin and her car were beyond saving. In full gear, one hurried in their direction.

"I'll be right back," Holden said, and Grace nodded. He climbed out to speak with the firefighter, who just happened to be his brother.

"Hey, what happened?" Sawyer asked.

"I was on my way here when I saw the cottage on fire."

Sawyer looked him over, his jaw clenching. "You went inside?"

"Yeah, how do you know?"

"There's soot on your face and clothes. Burn holes in your hat. What the hell were you thinking? You could've been killed."

Holden hadn't been thinking at all. His actions had been driven by pure instinct. "She was trapped inside. I had to get her out. If I had waited, she'd be dead."

Sawyer grunted, putting a boatload of frustration into the sound before he turned and whistled to one of the EMTs, waving him over. Then he hustled to the passenger's side of the truck with Holden right behind him. He opened the door and stood up on the footrail. "Hey, there, I heard you had a close call inside."

She nodded.

"Can you talk?" Sawyer asked. "I know the smoke and heat can hurt your throat. Can you tell me your name?"

"Grace." She swallowed like her throat was sore. "Grace Clark."

"So you're the one Holden is always going on about. Now I can see why my brother was reckless enough to run into a burning building."

Embarrassment sliced through Holden. With his family and his friends, he was a talker, like his mother. Perhaps he was guilty of oversharing, but no one could ever accuse him of being a closed book.

"Brother?" Grace asked, flicking a glance from Sawyer to Holden. "I thought you said all your brothers were in law enforcement."

"I don't like the sound of that rasp. Don't talk," Sawyer said. The EMT came around to the passenger's side, carrying a medical bag and blankets. Sawyer took the kit from him, pulled out an oxygen mask and fit it to her face. Next, he attached a small device to her finger. A pulse oximeter that measured the amount of oxygen in the blood. "To answer your question, I will be," Sawyer said. "I recently graduated from the fire marshal academy and I'm waiting to start in the position."

Once Sawyer began work officially as a fire marshal, he would be a sworn-in law enforcement officer, straddling the line between firefighting and police work, mostly investigating the causes of fires. Such as this one.

Which begged the question, who on earth had started it and why?

The EMT handed Holden a blanket.

"This is Pete," said Sawyer to Grace, trading places with the EMT on the footrail. "He's going to get your vitals and see if you need to go to the hospital."

She nodded as Pete draped a blanket over her legs and then he took out a blood pressure cuff.

Sawyer put a hand on his shoulder and hauled him a few feet away. "Any idea how the fire started?"

"Not for certain, but I think you'll find signs of arson," Holden said. "See if her smoke detectors were tampered with. They never went off. Also, she said the bedroom window had been nailed shut."

"I take it the window wasn't like that before tonight."

"No nails in it when I was there last night."

Sawyer quirked a brow. "Two nights in a row, huh?" his brother said with a wink, and Holden wanted to explain that it wasn't like that, but he decided not to waste his breath. "You better wake Mom and tell her what's going on before she hears it from someone else. Word spreads like wildfire. No pun intended."

His brother was right. Their father wouldn't be upset if he didn't learn about the fire until tomorrow because no one was hurt, but their mother preferred to be the first to know.

Since Pete was still examining Grace, listening to her breathing with a stethoscope, he took out his phone and got it over with.

When he was done filling her in, she said, "Thank heavens everyone is okay. Sawyer will get to the bottom of it. Poor Grace. She lost everything. You're bringing her to the ranch, aren't you?"

He hadn't thought about it, but that made sense to him. "Yeah, I suppose." He watched the firefighters trying to put out the blaze, the hose arcing a cascade of water onto the cottage.

"Will your *friend* be staying with you or in a guest room in the main house?"

Holden knew what she was really asking. "I don't know."

"I suggest you ask her and see what she wants."

"I will." All that mattered was Grace's comfort and safety.

"Holden, I need to tell you something and I want you to really listen to me."

"Okay. What is it?"

"You are loyal and steadfast. An honorable man who keeps his word. Just like your father. But the best thing about you is your heart. It's so big and you've got so much to give. It's time to move out of the shadow that Renee and Jim left behind. The people of this town have a long memory and will not soon forget until they have something more salacious to sink their teeth into. But you can't wait for them to give you permission to move on with your life. You deserve to be happy. Now. All you have to do is stop fighting it. Do you understand what I'm saying?"

Holden looked over at Grace. Their eyes met, and his heart squeezed. "Yeah, Mom. I think I do. Thanks." Pete was wrapping up with Grace and Sawyer was moving in, putting a hand on her arm. "I've got to go."

Hanging up, he strode over to his truck. He slid in close to Grace, nudging his brother aside and replacing Sawyer's hand on her arm with his own.

"The oxygen saturation level in her blood is normal. Her pressure and pulse are both good," Pete said. "Her airway sounds clear, and the oxygen mask seems to have helped. No more cough. But if it returns or she starts wheezing or gets a headache, I'd recommend taking her to the hospital for a chest X-ray."

"What about Holden?" she asked. "Aren't you going to examine him, too?"

"I'm fine," he said. "I was only inside a few minutes."

Sawyer knocked his cowboy hat off and caught it.

"Your Stetson doesn't look fine." His brother thrust it against his chest and Holden took it, looking at the burn holes from the falling embers. "If you start coughing or—"

"I know the drill," Holden said.

With no further need for Pete, the EMT left them.

"Since you're homeless, I take it you'll be staying at the ranch," Sawyer said, his gaze bouncing between them.

Grace shook her head. "I don't want to impose. I could always stay at the B and B, since I don't have a car to get to work."

"The B and B will add up," Holden said, and with a grimace, she nodded in agreement. "We also don't know who tried to kill you by setting the fire."

"No place safer for you to be at than the ranch," Sawyer said.

There was a security system. His entire family would be there, they had ranch hands living in the bunkhouse, and they were all armed.

"I guess." Grace sounded uncertain. "If you're sure it wouldn't be an imposition."

"It's no trouble," Holden reassured her. "You can stay with me in my apartment or in a guest room in the main house. My mother would love to have you close. Riddle you with questions. Stuff you with food."

She laughed, and there was no sweeter sound to his ears. "That seems like it might be a lot."

"It will be," Holden and Sawyer said in unison.

She flashed a gut-wrenching smile. "I'm fine staying with you."

Sawyer gave him a discreet wink. "I'll see you later tonight, Grace, in about eighteen hours, for the Powell Christmas Eve gathering. I should have some answers for you both about the fire by then." Sawyer patted her blanket-covered knee.

Holden swatted his hand off her leg and closed the door. "See you later and keep your hands to yourself."

His brother waved him off. "Make sure she hydrates."

Holden climbed in behind the steering wheel and backed out of the driveway.

Grace stared at the burning cottage. "I can't believe it's all gone. The house. My car. Everything I brought with me from my old life." She turned to him. Fresh tears glistened in her eyes. "All my things."

"Everything you lost is replaceable. All that matters is that you're safe."

"That we both are." She whisked the tears away and sniffled. "Someone tried to kill me. Almost succeeded, too. I could've died in there."

"It might've been the Iron Warriors." Maybe Todd didn't think a threat was enough.

"They're not behind this. If it had been them, they would not have left any doubt in my mind that they caused the fire. Of that, I'm sure."

She had a point. The MC wanted their victims to know they were responsible.

"We're going to find whoever is behind this. Make sure they don't hurt you again." He held out his hand to her across the console and she took it, interlacing her fingers with his.

They had both survived, and he could no longer run from his feelings for Grace Clark.

All this time he thought he had simply been falling for her. His brain constantly reminding him of the reasons he couldn't be with her...but it was too late. He was invested. As strange as it sounded, what was in his heart for her far exceeded *like* and had careened into the dangerous territory of that other four-letter word. He was already a goner.

He wanted Grace to be a part of his life, with all her strength, beauty and determination. If she would have him. To be an anchor for her, that person to keep her from drowning or getting lost in a storm. Everyone needed that and he wanted to give it to her.

His love for her was a fierce thing that he was no longer capable of fighting.

Chapter Fifteen

The wrought iron gates, emblazoned with the ranch's shooting stars brand, slid open and they pulled through.

Holden drove down a long, tree-lined driveway illuminated by landscape lights, toward a massive house. The mansion looked as if it had been plucked from the pages of a magazine, leaving no doubt in her mind that his family had money.

He proceeded to point out the other buildings on the property. In addition to the main house there was the ranch manager's cottage, two small staff casitas, a bunkhouse for the ranch hands, a vehicle storage building along with game-processing area, stables and a recreational building that included a kitchen, bar, an arcade and exercise facility.

And then there was his brother Montgomery's house.

"Your parents built him a house?"

"They hope to build one for each of us on the property, provided our spouses are amenable to the idea. Monty was engaged. Mom and Dad wanted the house ready by the wedding. But it wasn't meant to be." Holden shook his head. "So he lives there alone."

"Oh my goodness," she mumbled under her breath.

"What?" he asked.

"Why didn't you tell me your family is rolling in dough? I told you all about Selene."

"It's because of your mother that I thought none of this would make a difference to you."

She wasn't impressed or swayed by money. It was the exact opposite. "I spent my whole life running away from champagne wishes and caviar dreams." Her nerves were strung tight, making her babble. "Did I tell you that my mother tried to bribe me to fly home for Christmas with an eight-carat diamond tennis bracelet? And yours are building houses to keep their kids under their thumb."

"My parents don't use their money to lord it over us or try to control us. We're a close-knit family and we all help on the ranch. They worry that after they die we won't stay that way."

"I thought you came from salt-of-the-earth type of people. You know, laid-back and easygoing."

"We are. You know me." He pulled up by the two-car garage attached to the house and parked. "Look, it's been the worst night of your life. I get that your emotions are heightened, and this is a sensitive issue, but it shouldn't be one to concern you. This," he said, gesturing around at the buildings, "is nothing like the glamour and excess of what you came from in LA. We work from sunup to sundown." He held out his palm, putting his hand in her lap. "Those calluses aren't from writing reports at the sheriff's department," he said, and she ran her fingers over them, loving the rough feel of the hardened skin. "It's from busting my tail around here. You don't need to worry, Grace. I wouldn't have brought you if I thought you'd be uncomfortable here."

Everything felt like it was spinning out of control. Into some vortex that wanted to swallow her whole.

She took a deep breath and exhaled her fears before they spiraled further. She trusted Holden with her life. If anyone understood the torture of her childhood, it was him. As closely as she had listened to him, he had with her as well. "I'm sor—"

"Nope," he said, cutting off her apology.

"I'm feeling raw. Overwhelmed. I saw all of this, and I overreacted." It wasn't like her to jump to conclusions. To judge a book by its cover. She was having an out-of-body experience.

"Completely understandable. This has been a rough day."

"That's an understatement."

"Let me come around and get you." He walked to her side, helped her down to the foottrail and scooped her into his arms without letting her feet touch the ground.

Mounting the exterior stairs, he held her closer, and she wrapped her arms around his neck. The frigid night air prickled her bare legs since she had left the blanket in the truck.

He carried her up to his apartment. Opening the door, which he apparently kept unlocked, he brought her inside and set her down. Her gaze swept over the apartment as he rushed around, picking up things here and there. His place wasn't messy or dirty, just lived-in.

The apartment was spacious and well-designed. It

had an open floor plan. Hardwood floors throughout. White cabinets and black quartz countertops in the eat-in kitchen. No dining room, but the place didn't need one. He was a bachelor.

Any dinner parties he wanted to host for friends he could hold in the *recreation building.*

A cognac-colored leather sofa dominated the living room and faced a large-screen television.

"The bedroom is in here," he said, leading her to the room in the back. The bed was large and made and looked comfy.

There were little touches in his place, the art chosen, the finishes, the furniture, that elevated the space, making it seem as though it had been decorated by an interior designer. "Did your mom do your place or hire someone?"

"Yeah, she did it herself."

"She has a good eye," Grace said.

"Just so you know, I was planning to sleep on the sofa. Unless you didn't mind sharing the bed. I don't want to make you uncomfortable."

Warm blue eyes connected with hers as she smiled up at him. "It's fine."

A grin tugged at the corner of his mouth, bringing out a dimple to tease her. "Which one? Me sleeping on the sofa, or with you?"

With an amused snort, she said, "With me. You make me feel safe. Not uncomfortable. And I think we've proven that we can share a bed."

"I suppose we have." He leaned against the wall.

"Well, then, I promise to keep my hands and mouth to myself this time."

But she wasn't so sure that was a promise she wanted him to keep. Resisting Holden was a constant struggle. One she sensed herself finally ready to lose.

Her body urged her to close the small space between. There was nothing but honesty and desire in his expression, and all she wanted was to kiss him. To be held by him.

To make love to him.

"Let me show you to the bathroom." He dropped his gaze. "I'm sure you want to get cleaned up."

Soot coated her skin, and the smell of smoke permeated her nightgown and hair. "I could use a shower."

He brought her into the en suite bathroom. The tile and stonework were masculine, but there was still enough airiness to it that it was spa-like. The skylights would provide tons of natural light in the daytime. After showing her where he kept his things, he turned and started the large shower that had smooth stone flooring and two showerheads.

She took off his sheriff's jacket and handed it to him.

He glimpsed her in her nightgown, his gaze lingering as that warmth swept over again. Then he blinked several times before heading for the door.

"I'll uh—" he cleared his throat "—I'll get you something to wear." He left, closing the door behind him.

Quickly, she stripped off the nightgown and socks.

The hot water sluiced over her skin, loosening the knots in her muscles. At first, the water ran gray as it rinsed the soot from her skin. She'd gotten so lucky. The

EMT didn't think there was any damage to her lungs. He'd found no soot in her nose or throat.

Thanks to Holden, she was alive and well.

With no other choice, she used his shampoo and bodywash, but she took an odd pleasure in the thought of smelling like him. Cedar and sandalwood.

She didn't take too long, knowing he would want to shower as well. While she was towel-drying, he knocked on the door and opened it. He then came in, barely giving her a chance to cover herself with the towel.

"Sorry," he said, holding out some clothes, staggering to a stop. His gaze raked over her, his eyes heating with interest.

She took the T-shirt and boxer shorts he offered. "Thank you." At her words, he seemed to snap out of his daze with a shake of his head.

Diverting that mesmerizing gaze of his, he glanced down at the floor. "I'll get you some water." As he turned to leave, he almost bumped into the door, but managed to avoid a collision in the nick of time and shut it behind him.

After she threw on the clothes, which hung on her figure, she finger-combed the long, damp tangles out of her unruly brown waves. The entire time she wished for a wide-tooth comb. And a diffuser. And her hair products, without which she had no hopes of winning the battle to tame her rebellious curls. In the morning, her coils would be a frizzy hot mess.

After the horrors of the night that were still churning in her brain it shouldn't bother her. But it did.

Because she was with Holden, and she wanted to be at her best.

Not look her worst.

She was too weary to give it much more thought. It paled in comparison to the fact that they both could have died tonight.

"You're alive," she whispered to herself in the mirror, putting everything in proper perspective.

The rest didn't matter—that she was homeless, had lost all her possessions, her wallet, even her phone.

It was time she started living and stopped making excuses. Moving here to Wyoming was a good start, despite what was going on, but in a strange way, she realized her troubles had also brought her closer to Holden. Opened her eyes to what had been right in front of her all along.

Every time she was near him, he made her feel capable and beautiful. She was tired of not giving in to that magnetic draw, that sizzling heat he sparked with a single look.

Life was too short not to act on something that was special and real and true.

She stepped out into the bedroom.

He brought her a glass of water. "Here you go. I also set out a Gatorade for you. Grape. It was the only other option besides orange, and I know you don't like that flavor."

"Thank you."

"I'm going to shower."

She nodded. Turning, she headed for the living room.

"Grace," he said from the doorway, and she looked

back at him. "I love that you don't need makeup or anything. I mean, you're a natural beauty. Even after nearly
dying, you, well, you take my breath away."

Her face heated and the butterflies were back. She
swallowed hard against that deep, blossoming attraction tugging at her. Before she had a chance to respond,
he ducked into the bathroom and started the shower.

He knew just the right thing to stay. To put her at
ease. To make her feel sexy. She had always wanted
that in a guy, someone who didn't need the pretense
and flash. Someone who could see her at her worst and
still think she was beautiful.

She sipped the water, letting the cool liquid slide
down her parched throat. Once again, it was what she
needed. She hadn't realized she was so thirsty. She finished the entire glass and turned to the Gatorade. The
electrolytes hit the spot, refreshing her body the way
the shower had soothed her mind.

While the shower ran, she took in his apartment.
Looking over things more closely. His magazine sub-
scriptions on the table. What food he had in the fridge
and his pantry. Family pictures and artwork displayed
on the walls.

It painted a different picture of him. One she could
see herself fitting into.

The shower stopped and a moment later the bathroom door swung open. He came into the bedroom
wearing just a towel wrapped around his waist.

Air stalled in her throat. He was really good-looking,
so ridiculously male that her belly did a long, slow roll.

Tanned, well-muscled chest. Sculpted arms.

Beads of water glistened in his hair. She found herself staring and couldn't stop.

"I forgot to bring something to change into in the bathroom with me," he said.

She smiled. "It's okay. It's your house." Her mouth went dry. "I need some more water." She held up the glass and headed for the door.

He strode around the bed toward the closet on her side. "You've got to stay hydrated."

As they crossed the space, they found themselves face-to-face in the middle of the room at the foot of the bed. She stepped to the right while he went in the same direction at the same time, their movements keeping them in lockstep. They both smiled. Tried again, only to find themselves still eye to eye.

"Thanks for letting me bunk with you," she said, her voice sounding husky to her ears.

"Of course." His gaze fell over her, hot and intense. "You look good in my clothes."

"You look better out of them." She had no idea where that came from. The truth had simply slipped from her lips.

Her heart picked up a pounding pace, desire sliding through. She wanted him to kiss her. As she had the other night, but this time she didn't want anything to hold either of them back.

His gaze dipped to her mouth, but he tensed as though intending to keep his earlier promise of not touching her. So she stepped closer, her feet in between his, the T-shirt she wore brushing against his towel. He put a palm to her cheek, his thumb stroking across her lower lip, making her thighs quiver.

She had never experienced this kind of need before and couldn't stand it any longer. Sliding her hands in his hair, she rose on her toes, but he was the one to bring his mouth to hers.

The kiss was soft and sinfully sweet, aimed straight at her heart, until she slipped her tongue passed his lips and delved deeper. His arms came around her, pulling her against him while he shuffled their bodies back into the doorway with her spine to the jamb.

Just as she surrendered to him, no longer fighting her feelings, there was a quick rap at the front door and then it opened. They jerked apart as his mother strode in.

"Oh my," Holly said. "I, uh, I didn't mean to intrude."

Did all the Powells make a habit of knocking and entering a room without waiting for a response?

Holly looked as embarrassed as Grace felt. "I only popped over to give you some essentials, honey." Wearing a robe tied closed over her pajamas and boots, she came deeper into the apartment and handed Grace a wicker basket that had a white terry cloth robe rolled up, a new toothbrush, deodorant, a ladies' disposable razor, a boar's head brush, scented lotion, an organic ooh-la-la face cream that Selene would've approved of, mascara and lip balm. There were even a few sprigs of a plant that had waxy white berries, tied in a bundle with a red bow.

"This is so sweet of you. Thank you. Did you put this together just now?"

Holly nodded. "Oh, that's nothing, considering you've lost absolutely everything."

Grace held up the plant and smelled it, but it didn't have a scent. "What is this? It's so pretty."

"Mistletoe," Holly said with a mischievous smile. "But you two clearly don't need it. I'm never wrong about these things."

"Mom." He shook his head with an annoyed expression. "You're subtle as a sledgehammer."

Holly ignored him. "Holden will give you my phone number. I want you to text me a long list of things you need. I'm going to go to the store, first thing in the morning, to get you some shoes, boots, clothes, a coat. You're so tiny I don't have anything that would fit you. Please, if there is anything you want me to pick up, let me know. No matter what it is. There is no shame between us ladies. We've got to stick together with all these men around." Holly leaned in and gave her a quick, tight hug. "Seriously. I expect a *long* list, or I'll just hound you for one."

"She will," Holden said.

Grace believed them. She would've protested about the shopping since she didn't take well to charity, but she was in dire straits, with only a nightgown and a pair of socks to her name. It would take a couple of days to get her debit and credit cards replaced before she'd be able to buy anything on her own. "Thank you. That's very generous. I'll reimburse you for everything."

She might have to take out a small personal loan to do so, but she didn't want to be indebted to anyone.

"Don't be silly," Holly said. "It's the least we could

do. I'm glad you're okay. Both of you." She hurried to the door. "As you were. Go back to what you two were doing before I interrupted." The door closed. On the other side, Holly gave a little *woo-hoo* of cheer.

Grace couldn't fight back a smile, and neither could Holden.

"Your mom seems pretty fantastic."

"She is. In small doses."

Chuckling together, they went into the bedroom. She set the basket on the nightstand and turned to him.

"Grace, about that kiss." The hesitation in his voice made her get closer to him, erasing the distance. "The last few days have been traumatic for you. Downright awful. Maybe it's best for us to take a step back."

Her gut clenched. "You sound like you don't want this." Unease twisted through her. "Like you don't want me."

Had she read him and the mood wrong? Was it his mother walking in on them? Did he just want a secret friends-with-benefits arrangement?

"Don't want you?" Holden groaned. "You have no idea what you do to me. I want this with you more than I've wanted anything. It's just that you've been through a lot, and I shouldn't take advantage."

She put her hand on his bare chest, and he trembled beneath her palm. "Yes. You really should."

Still, he hesitated. "I love you, Grace. I don't want to mess this up by rushing. And I won't pretend that this is just sex for me because it isn't. It's more."

She stared at him dumbfounded, her heart thrumming, her blood singing, her mind spinning around the three words he'd declared.

I. Love. You.

"I don't want you to regret this in the morning," he continued. "I won't be able to hide how I feel or minimize it. You're not worried you'll wish we had waited?"

"No," she said on a breath as light as a caress. "I almost died. I almost lost this chance." To be with him and hear those precious words uttered straight from his heart. "The only thing I would regret is if you don't make love to me tonight." She ached to have him.

His sky blue eyes glinted and then his lips crashed hard into hers, kissing her like there was no tomorrow. He grabbed her by the hips and brought her down on the bed with him, their limbs in a tangle that had his towel falling to the side. She wanted to explore him, see all of him, feel him, taste him. But he flipped her onto her back and was on her again, his mouth as hungry for hers as though they had waited years for this instead of six months.

Six long months they'd spent getting to know each other, sharing, confiding, flirting, falling so hard that they hadn't even realized what was happening.

She tore her mouth from his, capturing his face in her hands, and stared in his eyes. "I love you." Her heart swelled to overflowing. "This is more for me, too."

"Good. I'm happy to hear that." He grinned, and there were those dimples that made her knees go weak.

He pressed his lips to her throat. His teeth scraped lightly against the tendon running up the side of her neck and then he was kissing her again.

Every nerve ending flamed, stoking the need to have him. She matched his ferocity with her own, forgetting to breathe as he stripped the clothes from her body. Closing her eyes, she wanted to drink in every sensation of what was about to happen.

Finally. Making love with Holden Powell while knowing that he loved her so much that he'd do anything to protect her. Even run into a burning building for her.

She took it all in, the scent of arousal, the heat they generated, the feel of his calloused hands on her sensitive skin everywhere he touched, the taste of him on her tongue. She moaned from the bittersweet pleasure, wanting to drown in the sensations.

More. She wanted so much more.

And he gave it to her.

Chapter Sixteen

The morning of Christmas Eve was, in a word, *amazing*.

Holden held Grace close, his fingers tracing over the curve of her hip. Her head was on his chest, her fingers playing in his hair, her slender leg draped over his thigh, her naked body pressed against his bare skin. He had never been happier.

After a passionate night, they snuggled in bed until a decadently late hour. Xavier had her set of keys from closing the previous night and was able to open Delgado's. Holden found himself actually thanking Judge Don Rumpke for insisting on issuing the warrant later in the day.

"I never thought it was possible to feel like this," she said, her breath brushing across his skin, tickling his chest hairs.

He stroked her wild curls back from her face. "Like what?"

"Everything is right in the world. Perfect. Just because I'm with someone who gets me, loves me as much as I love him, makes me feel safe. I know you have my back no matter what and it..." Her voice was no more than a breathy whisper as it trailed off. "It's hard to put into words."

He understood. The deep connection. The serenity it brought. The exhilaration. The hunger. "I get it. I feel the same." For the first time in his life. Like he could stay here in this one-bedroom apartment forever with her and not need anything else.

"The great sex doesn't hurt, either," she said, smiling.

"Great, huh?"

"Well, it was for me." The enthusiasm in her voice dimmed. "I haven't been with many guys. And my ex, Kevin, told me I wasn't very good at it and that he wouldn't miss it when we broke up."

Instantly, Holden hated a man that he had never met. "He said that to you?"

"Kevin said a lot of mean things at the end. In bed, he was always in such a rush, so forceful, like the only pleasure he cared about was his own. It didn't feel good."

His father had told him, and the rest of his brothers, that it was important for a man to take his time with a woman. That the longer he spent making certain she was ready the better it would be for them both.

He'd made sure that Grace had been more than ready and had relished teasing her, drawing out her pleasure like warm honey from a comb.

In the future, every time they were together, he wanted her to enjoy it as much if not more than him.

"Kevin sounds like an idiot. Any man who knows what he's doing understands that foreplay is half the fun. Not an appetizer that could be skipped."

She laughed. "What about you, Mr. All-State Football Star? I'm sure you've probably had better."

It was easy to have sex, and yes, he had experience, but with Grace it was different, more than physical. He made love to her with his whole heart.

"For the record, I haven't. Nothing has ever come close to what I have with you. On any level." He caught her chin in his hand and tipped her face up. "God, you're so beautiful." He kissed her and she sank into it, clutching him, gliding her hands over his body, in his hair, in every way possible drawing him deeper, closer until he craved being inside her again.

A sensation he would've liked to experience a lot longer. But a knock at his front door ripped a groan from him.

"One minute," he called out before going back for another quick kiss.

He wanted an hour or twelve. Hell, since he was fantasizing, he might as well wish for a whole day of Grace without any distractions, no interruptions.

But that was not to be.

Holden pulled himself out of bed, grabbed a pair of sweatpants and walked through the living room as he tugged them on. Bracing for the slap of cold wind, he opened the door.

His mother stood on the landing with her hands full of shopping bags. "Sorry it took me so long, but I went to Cheyenne. Better stores."

"It's fine." Too bad she didn't drive to Casper. It would've bought him more time with Grace. Not as though she could go to work without any clothes.

"I can see that." His mother beamed. "I love being right."

"I know you do."

"Take Grace's Christmas gifts." She handed him the bags. "I got everything on her list and then some. Do you want me to send up some food for you two?"

"No, thanks. I'll cook something quick." He held up the bags. "You're the best, Mom."

She kissed his cheek, waved and hurried down the steps.

Kicking the door closed, he headed to the bedroom. He dumped the bags on the bed.

"Goodness." Grace sat up. "Holly went overboard."

"Is that possible considering you have to replace everything?"

"I just can't afford all this."

Holden sat on the bed and put a hand on her back. "Hey, my mom knows how important you are to me. You're family. She'd be insulted if you tried to pay her back. So I guess you're stuck with all this stuff. Merry Christmas."

She flashed him a dazzling smile that never failed to give him a punch to the gut.

"Why don't you shower and dress while I cook us something to eat? I need to go in soon. I'm expecting Judge Rumpke to sign the warrant."

"You cook?"

"As a matter of fact, I do. My mother made sure all her boys know how to cook, clean, do laundry *and* sew. I'll never be a tailor, but I can mend my socks and put a button back on a shirt."

"I'm impressed." She gave him a kiss.

"As well you should be. How does pancakes and eggs sound?"

"Delicious."

"Hey." He caressed her cheek, letting the humor fade from his face. "Once I'm finished dealing with Todd, we're going to figure out who tried to kill you. Until we do, I don't want you closing Delgado's alone." She was staying at the ranch, and he was driving her to and from work, but there was still a window of opportunity when she was vulnerable, and he wanted to close it. "Okay?"

"I can close and stay safe."

This was not a debate or a negotiation. Grace could be stubborn, but this was a fight he was going to win.

"Will you do it for me? To put my mind at ease. It'll be a whole lot easier to focus on work if I'm not worrying about you."

With a sigh of resignation, she nodded. "Okay. For you."

"Thank you." He kissed her cheek. "I'll pick you up from work at six. We'll have dinner with my family at seven, and you can meet everyone."

"I'm looking forward to it. I want to get to know them."

Relief seeped through him that she was going to use more caution and not close on her own and also that she wanted to be a part of his life.

He couldn't ask for anything more.

Now that that was resolved, he could enjoy what was to come next. Getting his warrant, then slapping handcuffs on Todd and hauling him in for formal questioning.

HOLDEN SLID THE evidence bag with the Shining Light necklace across the table in the interrogation room, putting it in front of Todd and his lawyer, Mr. Friedman. As soon as Holden had shown up with other deputies and the warrant, Todd had invoked his right to an attorney. They had to wait two hours for his lawyer to arrive to question him.

"We found that, Emma's necklace," he said, gesturing to it, "in our search of your room at your clubhouse. How did you come into possession of it?"

Whispers were exchanged between Todd and his lawyer before the outlaw biker said, "I don't recall."

"I saw those everywhere," Mr. Friedman said. "It's entirely possible that he stumbled upon one. There's no proof that it belonged to the deceased. My client had no motive to kill his sister. And I believe there's no eyewitness putting him at the scene of the crime, is there?"

"There's no witness that has identified Mr. Burk," Holden said. "We were able to obtain the warrant because your client lied about his alibi. I followed a hunch and have several witnesses as well as credit card receipts putting Nikki Adams in Cheyenne at the Wild Pony at the time your client claimed she was with him. And as to motive, he does have one."

Todd whispered in his attorney's ear.

Then Mr. Friedman smirked. "We'd like to hear this supposed motive."

Holden folded his hands on the table. "Emma was approaching the one-year anniversary of her rebirth."

"You mean brainwashing," Todd said, and his lawyer put a hand on his shoulder.

"In the days prior to the ceremony, Starlights share with Matthew McCoy all the nasty tidbits about their former life. Specifically related to people. Allegedly, McCoy uses that information to blackmail those who aren't members. It's my understanding that Emma had intimate knowledge regarding the illicit activities of the Iron Warriors. It would only make sense that Todd would want to silence her."

More whispering ensued as the two conferred.

"The Iron Warriors and the Shining Light have an understanding," Mr. Friedman said, straightening his tie. "They stay out of each other's way. As for blackmail, well," he chuckled, "no one has ever successfully extorted the Iron Warriors. I think they'd welcome anyone to try. Besides, Emma was a known junkie, liar and a thief among other things. Anyone who took her word as gospel regarding anything and tried to capitalize off it would've been a fool."

Todd smiled.

That piece of garbage thought he was going to win and walk out of there triumphant.

Holden hated him with a passion and would do anything, within legal bounds, to nail him.

In their sophomore year of high school, one of his best friends had witnessed Todd dealing drugs on the school premises and reported it. Before the sheriff's department had a chance to investigate, his friend was found dead. Beaten to death.

The authorities couldn't prove it was Todd, but everyone at school knew he had been responsible.

That was when Holden had decided that one day, he

would become a law enforcement officer to put a stop to scum like Todd.

He hoped that the day of reckoning had finally come.

Holden flipped the bag over, showing the other side of the necklace. "When someone is reborn a Starlight and gifted this," he said, tapping the pendant, "their name is engraved on the back of the medallion. There are many like it, but only one belongs to each Starlight. And this one is Emma's. I also have an eyewitness who saw her wearing it less than two hours before she was killed."

Todd's smile slipped from his face. His black eyes narrowed and his jaw clenched.

Mr. Friedman shrugged. "That's circumstantial."

"Her killer," Holden said, "was riding a black motorcycle that night—"

"So what?" Mr. Friedman said, cutting him off. "Do you know how many people ride a black Harley around here? Do you have a witness who saw his bike? His license plate?"

They kept fishing, wanting him to imply the sheriff's department had Grace as a witness.

That bait wouldn't work on Holden. There was nothing they could say that would cause him to endanger her.

"No, we don't," Holden said, which was true since she never saw a license plate, "and we don't need one. Because we have forensic evidence from the scene. The motorcycle scraped a parked car as it fled, and paint was transferred. Once we verify that it came from your client's motorcycle and along with this—" he held up the bag with the necklace "—we'll move from circumstantial to concrete. Then you can expect the district attorney's office to file formal charges for obstruction of justice, giving false statements to the sheriff's department when questioned, fleeing the scene of an accident that resulted in injury," he said, clenching his fist at how Grace had almost been killed, "and of course, murder." This time Holden smiled. "There's one more thing. We know Emma called her killer from a pay phone. All we have to do is request the records." And wait until the cows come home. "Once we get them, this case will be airtight."

Todd went still with a suddenly unreadable expression, but the concern in his eyes was plain to see. He leaned over and whispered to his lawyer. The more Todd said, the more Mr. Friedman's grimace deepened.

"Well, yes, that's possible," Mr. Friedman said in a low voice, in response to his client, "to save on resources."

Todd resumed whispering furiously.

"What?" Mr. Friedman said, shrinking back with alarm and looking at Todd. "You can't."

"Yes, I can." Todd scowled at his attorney, and Holden wondered what was unfolding in front of him.

Mr. Friedman put a hand on his client's shoulder. "It would be a mistake to do this. There are other ways to handle it."

Todd shoved the older man's hand away and straightened. "I'd like to confess."

Surprise knocked Holden back in his chair, the shock gripping the pit of his stomach like a cold fist.

"I must advise against this." Mr. Friedman's voice

grew frantic. "Don't say anything else. Not another word. Do you hear me?" The lawyer turned to Holden. "He doesn't know what he's saying. He's confused. I need a minute to confer with my client in private. Right this instant."

Holden stood to leave, per protocol. The two were allowed to speak in complete privacy, with the sound shut off in the observation room and video recording halted.

"We don't need a minute to talk," Todd said.

Holden didn't take another step toward the door and stayed planted where he stood.

"Yes, we do," Mr. Friedman insisted, his face reddening. "You pay me a lot of money for my legal advice. I urge you to heed it now by shutting up!" His attorney cut his gaze to Holden. "Get out and let us talk. Or I will file a complaint against this department and have your badge."

Todd leaned forward, resting his arms on the table, and stared Holden straight in the eyes. "It was me. I killed Emma."

Chapter Seventeen

After letting all that Todd Burk had said sink in and considering everything, it still didn't sit well with Holden. He ordered the forensic testing of Todd's motorcycle to be expedited, bumped up from days to hours. Then he called in the assistant district attorney, Melanie Merritt, to get her opinion since it would be her office who would file formal charges if they decided to go forward on this.

She didn't hesitate to come straight over on a Sunday, on Christmas Eve. The ADA's reputation for being a workaholic was panning out to be true.

In his opinion, Todd's admission stunk to high heaven. He couldn't put his finger on why it was fishy, but he was determined to get to the bottom of it.

Melanie had looked at the evidence found in the execution of the warrant and watched the recorded playback of the interview. Now she was standing quietly in the observation room, watching them.

"He confessed," Ashley said. "On video. We should be celebrating."

"That would be premature," Holden said. Todd's supposed confession didn't put him in a festive mood. On the contrary, it left him uneasy.

Mitch entered the room and hesitated as he picked up on the tension. Then he caught Holden's eye. "Nurse Tipton from the hospital called. Emma Burk's records are ready. She's got them at the nurses' station where she's working today, if you still want to talk to her."

Holden gave him a nod of thanks as Mitch joined them.

Ashley stormed up to Holden. "We can't just ignore what he told us. Right?" She looked to the ADA, who remained silent and observant.

Melanie wasn't the type to weigh in quickly or lightly. She made it a point of doing a thorough assessment first before sharing her thoughts and only got her office involved if she believed they could win a case.

Her silence spoke volumes, meaning she had doubts as well.

"I'm not saying we should ignore it." Holden folded his arms and stared through the one-way glass. Todd and his attorney were no longer embroiled in a heated discussion. Mr. Friedman had stormed out of the sheriff's department to make a few calls on his client's behalf. No doubt to find a way to get Todd off the hook.

"Then what are you saying?" Mitch asked, trying to play catch-up after missing the last ten minutes of discussion.

"Why did Todd confess?" Holden wondered aloud. "Who fights with their attorney, disregarding their advice in order to get themselves arrested and charged?" None of it made any sense.

Ashley sighed. "A guilty man. That's who."

"Maybe," Holden said with a shrug. Maybe a guilty man with a conscience, but that wasn't Todd.

In the interview room, Todd sat still as stone, staring at the one-way glass like he wasn't worried about a thing. "This doesn't feel right. Something about it is off. Wrong."

Ashley responded with a loud groan. "Do you know how many people Todd Burk and the Iron Warriors have hurt in this town?"

"I'm not keeping a running tally," Holden said, "but I know it's a hell of a lot."

"Do you understand the damage he's caused?" She pinned him with her gaze. "The families he's torn apart with his drugs and guns and violence?" Tears glistened in her eyes.

If anybody in the sheriff's department wanted to see Todd locked up behind bars for the rest of his life more than Holden, it was Ashley.

His best friend in high school had been Angelo Russo. Her older brother.

Holden believed Angelo's murder had driven her to join the sheriff's department the same as him. They had never spoken about it—his friendship with Angelo, the hole that his death had left behind, their mutual hatred for the person responsible—but whenever Todd's name came up, something dark flashed in her eyes, the haunted look reminding him of her family's devastation.

Turning away from the observation room, Holden faced her. "I realize what he's taken from you and your family. Believe me, I want him." So badly that his gut burned with the need to stop that man from hurting anyone else and to see justice served.

"This is a win," Mitch said. "We should take it. Why look a gift horse in the mouth?"

Holden took a calming breath. "Because this gift horse might turn out to be a Trojan horse instead."

"How so?" Melanie asked, speaking for the first time.

If only he knew. That was the answer they needed to understand why this admission of guilt couldn't be trusted.

"He confessed to murder!" Ashley said. "Finally, we have him."

"Let's think about this." Holden kept his tone calm and firm, determined to keep this precarious situation in perspective. "For the past fourteen years, that man," he said, pointing through the observation window at Todd, "has beaten all charges brought against him for everything from possession, drug dealing, arms trafficking, rape, domestic violence and murder. He struts around acting like he's untouchable. The Iron Warriors call him Teflon for a reason. But today he chooses to confess, against his attorney's advice." He exhaled his frustration. "I'm telling you this isn't a reason to jump for joy. It's cause for concern."

"Maybe you're overthinking it," Ashley said. "Maybe you backed him into a corner, and he realized there was no other way out." Her voice tightened with desperation. "The judge could give him a lighter sentence because he confessed. Isn't that true?" she asked the ADA.

Melanie nodded. "It is. If he were to plead guilty rather

than get convicted at trial, he could receive a lesser plea sentence."

But that was not nearly enough justification for Todd to admit to murder. The composed man sitting in the other room didn't look like someone who was prepared to do any jail time.

Then the dots suddenly connected, coming together for him. "You're right, Ashley, there is no way around the evidence, and he knows it. That's why he confessed, but not because he's guilty."

"What are you saying? He did it just to confuse things and complicate the investigation?" Ashley asked. "But why?"

"It's because he's protecting someone. The real killer."

Ashley shook her head. "I don't understand. Why would he risk prison to protect someone else? The only person he cares about is himself."

"That's not true," Holden said. "Like most of us, he cares about his family and would do anything for them. But in the long run, he's not risking prison."

"How would he wiggle out of a conviction after telling us point blank that he committed murder?" Ashley asked.

"Oh, he's a smart devil," Melanie said, in a low voice, almost to herself. "Very clever." She stepped forward, a smile tugging at her lips. "How would a man who didn't do the crime yet confessed that he did avoid a guilty verdict? With a mistrial."

"But how can he hedge his bets that he'd get one?" Mitch asked.

Melanie folded her hands. "Let's say you believed

his confession. What would the sheriff's office do at this point besides celebrate?"

Holden sighed. "Try to corroborate his confession."

"But really, you'd only be going through the motions," Melanie said. "Everyone wants him to be guilty. You all have been trying to pin something to him for years. Once you have enough to tick the box, you'd happily leave it alone if for no other reason than to save on resources."

Ashley's eyes lit up. "That's what his attorney said. Those exact same words, *save resources*, when he was answering one of Todd's questions."

"If Todd refused a plea deal and decided not to plead guilty when this was brought in front of a judge, then it would go to trial. My office," Melanie said, "wouldn't realize we couldn't win the case until it was too late after we entered discovery." The formal process of exchanging information between the parties about the witnesses and evidence that would be presented at trial. "If he didn't do it, then he knows there's either evidence or a witness or both that will trigger a mistrial. Any idea what that might be?"

"We should hear back soon from the lab on paint analysis since I asked them to put a rush on it," Holden said. "Todd seemed worried about us running the forensics. I think that means it won't match. And he might have a real alibi besides the Iron Warriors who'd lie for each other. There were strippers at the clubhouse the night of the murder. Supposedly he's got a favorite. Her name is Misty. He might have been with her at the time in question."

"I'll go talk to her," Mitch volunteered.

Melanie stepped closer, catching Holden's gaze. "I watched the playback of your interview three times. You're right that Todd's whole demeanor changed when you mentioned the forensics. This confession of his would give the real killer an opportunity to fix whatever mistake they made regarding the paint."

Holden nodded. "But it wasn't until I talked about the records from the pay phone that he got scared. There's no way to cover that up."

"Then this charade will give that person a chance to run," Melanie said. "Who do you think Todd is protecting?"

"Someone he cares about. Someone he would do anything for. Todd's parents were worried about losing their granddaughter to Emma. His father was furious about the custody battle and said it would've been better if Emma hadn't survived the last time she had OD'd. I think he's protecting Gary Burk."

QUESTIONING GARY WOULD TAKE FINESSE. Without the records from the pay phone, which could take months for them to receive, they had nothing. While Todd had time on his side and in turn was giving Gary a chance to run.

Holden needed Gary to slip up and give something away so that they could hold him in custody and charge him. But to agitate the guy and break him down to the point of self-incrimination, Holden needed more information.

He strode up to the desk at the nurses' station.

Terri greeted him with a smile. "Hey, there, Holden."

She stood and handed him a thick manila envelope that had been sealed. "Those are the records on Emma Burk, and I heard you were looking for me."

"Yeah, can we speak? Somewhere privately?"

"Sure." She led him to a supply closet and closed the door. "What's up that requires such confidentiality?"

"I'm trying to get to the bottom of who killed Emma. I need to nudge a suspect, but I have to be sure I'm pushing the right buttons."

Her smile faltered. "Okay. But I don't know how I can help."

He sighed. "I'm not asking for details. I just need to know if the Burks have a tendency to come into the emergency room with accidents."

Terri narrowed her eyes at him. "I'm not sure I know what you're asking."

"Accidents that could possibly be abuse. Lorraine. Kyle."

She stiffened. "Please tell me you're not asking me to violate a federal law by disclosing HIPAA-protected medical information?"

"If you reasonably believe that either is a victim of abuse or domestic violence permitted disclosure is allowed. I'm not asking for any specifics, but if Lorraine has been coming in with black eyes or claiming she fell, I need to know."

"I've been working in the ER for years. The Burks aren't regulars. I know what an abused person and ongoing domestic violence looks like when I'm treating someone. Every time Todd's girlfriend ends up in here, I've reported it."

That was true. Holden sighed. "What about Kyle? He might not be a regular, but he came in a week ago for a broken hand. Maybe it wasn't an accident. I don't want you to disclose anything you're not comfortable with, but if Kyle's hand wasn't an accident, I need to know."

"I have never believed the rumors about you," she said. "You've always been a stand-up a guy, even in high school. But this—"

"Straddles the line. I know. I've got one chance at this. In a few hours, Todd Burk is going to be released because the DA's office isn't going to charge him. Then he's going to make a phone call and the real guilty person is going to get away. Please help me. All I want is justice for Emma. You knew her, didn't you? She was on the cheerleading squad with you before she got caught up in drugs."

Terri lowered her head. "Emma was just a freshman when she joined the squad." Her expression and demeanor softened. Sucking in a deep breath, she flicked a glance at the door. "Kyle claimed what happened to his hand was an accident. It's possible. But…" She hesitated. "It's also possible that it wasn't. What I can say for certain is that it didn't happen a week ago."

He rocked back on his heels. "What? Then when?"

"Kyle came into the ER early Friday morning."

After Emma was killed? "Are you sure?"

"It was after three thirty, close to four in the morning. He was the last person I helped the doctor treat before my shift ended. I'm positive."

PULLING UP TO Custom Gears, Holden answered an incoming call from Mitch. "What did you learn?"

"Misty was reluctant to talk, but I assured her it was to help Todd stay out of trouble and that for now her statement would be off the record."

"And?"

"She claims that she was with Todd most of the night. At first, they were partying with the other Iron Warriors, then she entertained him privately in his room from midnight to three in morning, when he got a call on his cell. Whatever it was about seemed to upset him and he left in a hurry."

"Thanks." Holden disconnected and strode into the office of Custom Gears. "I have some follow-up questions, if you don't mind," he said to Kyle.

"Sure." Kyle stood and came around the desk. "My parents are at home, making funeral arrangements for Emma. We can go over and talk together."

"That won't be necessary," Holden said as they stepped outside. "I'd rather not disturb them. Not when you can help me."

"Okay."

"Can we go to the garage and take another look at the motorcycles while we talk?" Holden asked.

Kyle shrugged. "If you want." Across the street, Kyle opened the garage.

As they entered, Holden pulled out his recorder and held it up. "Do you mind? It's so I don't have to take notes and it makes my report easier to complete."

"Whatever. Let's just get on with it."

Holden started the recorder. "Thanks for answering

a few follow-up questions. I know this is a difficult time for your family. When is the funeral?"

"A couple of days after Christmas."

"Hopefully, this will be my last visit."

"Anything I can do to help," Kyle said.

"Over at Custom Gears," Holden said, running a hand over the Fat Boy 114, "let's say this rear fender were to get damaged, scraped in an accident. How long to fix it, make it look brand-new?"

"I don't know. I've never timed it."

"Take a guess. What's the fastest do you think it could be done?"

Kyle shrugged. "Maybe, uh, two to three hours."

"When was the last time you saw Emma?"

"I already told you."

"I'm sorry to go over the same ground. If you wouldn't mind telling me again."

"Thursday night. Here at the house."

"Are you sure you didn't see her again later?"

Kyle tensed. "I'm sure."

"You were really worried about your parents, weren't you? About what Emma was putting them through with the custody battle."

"Yeah, of course I was."

Holden nodded. "I only have a couple more questions."

Cautious relief crept over Kyle. "Sure."

"First, I'm going to tell you what I've pieced together so far and then I just need you to fill in the blanks for me. I only have two left." Holden walked away from the motorcycle toward Kyle. "Emma fought with your parents, giving your mom a migraine, nearly giving your father a stroke. But you didn't get involved. You stayed on the sidelines, listening and watching. That's what made Emma feel comfortable enough to call you later for a ride back to the B and B."

"What?" Kyle's face turned pale. "She didn't call me. I wouldn't have picked her up after what she said to Mom and Dad."

"That's precisely why you did pick her up. Because you thought you'd talk some sense into her. Right? Get her to change her mind. But you two ended up fighting instead. The next thing you know you pushed her."

"Wearing this?" Kyle held up his broken hand, his mouth tightening in a hard, thin line. "I can't ride a bike wearing a cast."

"That's true. It's the reason I initially dismissed you. But both of your hands were fine when you killed Emma. Weren't they?"

His eyes went wide. "No!" Fury gripped Kyle's face. Then he tried to compose himself. "No," he said again in a calmer voice. "It was broken."

"And both your hands were fine when you repaired your father's bike, which took two to three hours. After that Todd came over and for some reason, somehow, he broke your hand."

Kyle made a guttural sound of outrage. "You don't know what you're talking about. You can't go around making up stories because you're too incompetent to do your job."

"What I can't figure out is why you called Todd and

how he ended up with Emma's Starlight necklace. Can you fill in those blanks for me?"

If looks could've killed, Kyle would've put Holden six feet under.

"I was home all night long," Kyle said through clenched teeth.

"You fixed the bike to erase the damage, but you're forgetting about the phone records. The call Emma made at the pay phone *to you*. You can't make it disappear."

Not expecting that, Kyle blinked in surprise, but he was still fuming, looking as if he was deciding between fight or flight.

"You found a way to circumvent the security system on the house," Holden continued, "or your dad knew you shut off the alarm and left, which would mean he lied to me. Maybe both your parents lied because they knew that you killed Emma. That's obstruction of justice. If I arrest your parents, Amelia will get thrown into foster care or maybe Jared will get her. Either prospect would be unthinkable, unbearable to your parents."

Kyle's expression shifted as he withered in front of him. "No, you can't do that. They didn't know. They had nothing to do with it."

"With what?" Holden eased closer. "Fill in the blanks for me. So we can leave Gary and Lorraine out of this. So Amelia can stay with them. Isn't that what you wanted all along?"

A broken sob came from Kyle. "I didn't mean to kill Emma. It was an accident."

"Tell me how it happened."

"She called me. Asked me to come get her because of the rain."

"Did you turn off the alarm?"

Kyle shook his head. "The security guy that installed it forgot to put a sensor on one of the windows in the basement. I like it that way. So I can come and go as I please."

"Your parents didn't know you left?"

"No." A single tear rolled down his eye.

"What happened with Emma?"

"She wouldn't listen to reason. Wanting to take a little kid into that compound. We don't know what goes on in there. I begged her," he said, with pleading eyes, "begged her to put a stop to the custody proceedings. But she was being so stubborn because McCoy got into her head. We fought. And I just…" Another sob came from him. "I just wanted her to stop. I put my hands around her throat and I," he said with a hiccup, "I squeezed and squeezed. I don't know." Kyle lifted a shoulder, his eyes glistening with tears. "I guess I pushed her. And then her necklace was in my hand. Then I ran."

"You were scared and had all that adrenaline pumping." Holden softened his voice. "You came back here."

Swallowing, Kyle nodded. "I saw the scrapes on the bike. I had to fix it. So Dad wouldn't see it and ask questions."

"Why did you call Todd?"

Kyle gave a hoarse sob. "I had to tell someone. I didn't know what to do."

"What happened when he came?"

Hanging his head, Kyle broke down, weeping. "I told

him what I did. Showed him the necklace. He snatched it from me. Called me stupid. Todd was so angry." Tears fell from his eyes. "He took a hammer and he smashed it on my hand."

"Why?"

Kyle clutched his broken hand, holding it to his chest. "I felt like it was to punish me. Then when you came around asking questions, I don't know, I thought maybe he did it so you wouldn't suspect me."

If that was the reason, it had worked.

"I've got to take you in, Kyle." Holden turned him around, took out zip ties and put the plastic cuffs on him that would fit over his cast. "You're under arrest for the murder of Emma Burk."

Chapter Eighteen

Strolling back to Delgado's from dropping off the last of their delivery orders for the night, Grace couldn't stop smiling. She was walking on cloud nine.

In one night, she had lost everything and gained so much more at the same time. The old had been purged, making way for the new. From the love that was overflowing in her heart down to her boots.

She never thought it was possible to be this happy. So much at peace with herself and her life.

Holden was such a good fit for her, and she hoped she was for him as well. Not only was he gorgeous and kind and sexy, he was a great lover and a terrific cook, too. His bacon had been a perfect mix of crispy and chewy, his pancakes fluffy and moist.

He didn't talk *at* her but *to* her, and he listened. No matter how scary or dark things got, he managed to be a beacon of light, brightening everything.

Why had they waited so long to get together?

Even her worries about what his family would be like had dissipated after she'd gone through the shopping bags Holly had dropped off. At first, the highlight had been seeing a bag filled with all the hair products from her list. But then she noticed his mother had removed the price tags from the clothes and had included a note saying she didn't want her to stress out about it. As Grace would have done. Holly had taken care to pick out simple, comfortable things that were flattering to her skin tone and figure while not being the least bit fancy. His mom hadn't tried to push off what she thought would be good for her.

As Selene would have done in such a situation.

Holly had managed to make her feel seen and accepted. Not judged. Not bribed. Simply overwhelmed in a good way with that kind act of generosity.

Grace would still find some way to pay them back without insulting anyone. Whether it was by helping on the ranch or doing her best to make Holden as happy as he was making her. Which in her book would be a win-win.

Before going into the restaurant, she pulled out the prepaid cell phone Holly had also gotten her. Grace had forgotten hers in the bathtub once she realized Holden had come to get her out of the burning house.

She texted her mother to let her know this was her new number. Then she gave her a quick call.

"Hello."

"Hi, Mom."

"Why do you have a new number?"

"It's a long story and I don't have time to get into it, but I wanted you to have it."

"Did something happen, Bug?"

So much over the past few days. She didn't want to

worry her mother with any of it, but with this second lease on life she'd been given she was going to live on her own terms. "Yeah, but I'll tell you about it tomorrow. Hey, Mom, when I was little and you used to call me Love Bug, it made me smile. Made me feel special. But I hate it when you shorten it to just *Bug*. It reminds me that I'm none of the things you ever wanted me to be. That I'm nothing like you. There are so many other things you could call me that are sweeter and nicer than that."

"Oh." Unnerving silence followed.

Selene was never quiet.

"Mom?"

"I'm sorry. I always thought of it as our verbal shorthand. That you knew *Love* was implied. Grace, I've never wanted you to be a mini me. One Selene Beauvais is enough."

Grace couldn't agree more.

"But I did want you to be better than me. That's what every parent wants. And in so many ways you are. You're my baby and you'll always be special, regardless of what I call. But I'll stick to *Love Bug*, not shorthand, or sweetie."

"Simply calling me Grace is fine."

"When have I ever settled for fine?"

She laughed. "I've got to get back to work, Mom. We'll talk later. Love you."

"Love you, too, Grace."

Smiling, she hung up and pushed through the door of Delgado's.

The dinner crowd was thinner than usual on a Sunday night thanks to it being Christmas Eve. Two more hours until Xavier closed early and less than one until

Holden picked her up so they could have dinner with his family.

As Xavier was walking a couple of plates to table ten, he stopped her. "Someone is here looking for you."

"Who?"

"Guy at the bar. He had a couple of drinks, settled his bill and he's just been waiting. Good tipper."

She turned to see, but there were lots of guys at the bar. "Which one?"

"At the end. Gray sweater," Xavier said, heading to table ten.

She glanced back and doubted her eyes. From the back, he looked familiar, but his hair was longer, shaggier. Not cropped to his collar.

But it couldn't be.

Grace walked around the bar and went behind it, and came face-to-face with Kevin Hughes.

She swayed, feeling hot and then cold. "What are you doing here?"

"Hello to you, too." He smiled, and she remembered that she had once found him attractive. His chestnut-brown hair was smooth and shiny and long enough now to be pulled in a man bun that would've fit in back in LA. "I'm waiting for you."

"No, I mean, what are you doing here in Wyoming?"

He finished his drink and set the glass down on his receipt. "My grandmother's estate finished going through probate. She left you something. I brought it for you, and I was hoping we could talk."

"About what?"

Kevin sighed. "I don't like the way we left things.

I want to make amends." He got up from the barstool and put on his jacket. "Can we go outside where it's quieter?" When she hesitated, he added, "I came a long way." He flashed a charming smile. "Please."

She did need to close this chapter in her life and move on so that she never thought about it or him again. Maybe this was her opportunity. "Yeah, sure."

He held the door open for her and she walked outside.

The door swung closed with a thud.

"How did you know I worked here?" she asked.

"Selene. It's driving her bananas that you're working as a waitress instead of using your nursing degree."

Of course. Her meddling mother had struck again. "I'm a manager, not a waitress, and I'm going to school, getting my master's."

"That's nice," he said, his tone dismissive. "I'm sorry for being a jerk at times." He shivered from the cold. "For the way I behaved when you ended it."

Like a petulant child having a tantrum because he didn't get what he wanted. Maybe he acted that way because his grandmother had spoiled him when he was little after his mother died. But there was no excuse for being mean. "And the things you said to me?"

"Oh, yeah. That, too. I was awful."

She couldn't disagree.

"But we had some good times together, didn't we?"

They had a shared love of art and that was how they had first connected. There were moments when he'd been nice and fun to be around, and others when he hadn't. "I guess we did."

"Come on, I want to give you what my grandmother

left for you." He stepped off the sidewalk into the parking lot.

"Go where?"

"Right over there." He pointed to the B and B.

"You're staying at the Quenbys'?"

"Can we go talk for a few minutes? I'm only in town for one night. I got in a little while ago and I fly out tomorrow from Denver. I won't keep you long. Five, ten minutes tops. I'm sure you've got plans."

It wasn't like him to think of anyone but himself, but he'd flown all the way out here with a quick turnaround. At Christmas. For ten minutes of her time?

"Okay." Putting her hands in her pockets, she walked with him.

He started making small talk, asking her questions about how she liked living out here. Her focus was torn as she answered. She couldn't help but think about Emma Burk and the night in the rain when the young woman had died.

Opening the front door of the B and B, he let her go in ahead of him.

It was quiet inside. Only a couple of side table lamps were on. "Are the Quenbys here?"

"They mentioned something about going to Christmas Eve mass. They left some cookies out on the table for me. Would you like some?"

"No, thanks."

He showed her up to his room, number two, and she wondered which one Emma had stayed in.

After letting her in, he closed the door. "Let me take your coat for you." He held out his hand and waited.

She slipped it off and gave it to him.

The room was large enough to accommodate a bed, a bistro-size table and two chairs. The lamp was on. But then her gaze flew to the candles burning and the bouquet of flowers on the dresser beside a bottle of wine and two glasses.

"Kevin, I hope you didn't ask me up here with romantic intentions."

"Before I show you what my grandmother left for you, I have a gift." He went to the dresser and grabbed a small box. As he turned to her, she noticed that it was a velvet ring box. He flipped it open, revealing a diamond ring, and knelt on one knee. "Grace, I know I'm not perfect and I've made a lot of mistakes. I'm a work in progress. But in this time apart, I've reflected and thought about you every single day. With your love and support, I can be a better man. One worthy of you. I know you think I was only interested in you for your mother's money, but that isn't true. I love you. Will you marry me?" Her eyes flared wide, and he continued, "Let's just throw caution to the wind and do it. We could be married in an hour. And to show you that I only want you, not Selene's money, I had a prenup drawn up. It states that anything you get from your mother is entirely yours. Put it in a trust. Something ironclad that I can't touch. I only want you."

Selene had told him that a grand gesture was required, and he thought a proposal was a good idea?

She was speechless. Not only had he managed to be humble while addressing her concerns, but it was also kind of sweet.

Like saccharin.

And just as artificial.

"No, Kevin. I can't marry you."

Hanging his head, he got up from the floor. "Is it because you don't believe me?"

ONLY PARTLY. "It's because I don't love you." She never had. What made it worse, she was embarrassed for herself that she had ever been taken in by him, settled for what little he had to offer.

"Well, I love you so much that I had to try." With a disappointed look, he closed the ring box and traded it for the bouquet of roses. "In case you said no, I still wanted to give you something. I really am sorry for everything."

Once again, surprise rocked through her. This was so unlike him. "Thank you." She took the flowers. "I can't stay long."

"Right." He grabbed the bottle of wine. "My grandmother wanted you to have this." He showed her the label.

It was a 1996 Petrus Pomerol. A $5,000 bottle of Bordeaux.

"Oh my goodness. I used to joke with her about trying it one day."

"She wanted to make sure you'd get that day. The rest of the case is being shipped to you."

"A whole case?"

"That's right, but I was hoping we could try a bottle together. One glass. You keep the rest." He must have sensed her hesitation, because he added, "We can toast to her." He held up the bottle. "I leave tomorrow morning. You'll never have to see me again. I think my grandmother would've liked it if we took a few minutes to honor her together over something she loved."

It was true. Miss Linda would've wanted them to make amends, celebrate her and then move on, going their separate ways with no ill will. "What time is it?"

He checked his watched. "Five thirty. Can you spare a few minutes for a quick glass?"

This was nice, like it was in the beginning between them, before they'd started dating. "One."

"Thanks. You were always such a sweetheart." Kevin pulled out a chair for her and she sat.

He went back to the dresser to open the bottle. "The Quenbys told me this is the best room in the B and B. It even has a view. Check it out."

She pulled back the curtain. He had a view all right. Of the mountains, the street and the rear of Delgado's. She got a creepy image of him sitting at the window, watching her take out the trash, opening and closing the restaurant. Goose bumps prickled her skin. "When did you get here?"

The cork squeaked out of the bottle. "Just today," he said with his back to her. Then there was the *glug, glug* sound of him pouring the wine. "I landed this afternoon and then drove up from Denver." Turning, he faced her, holding the two glasses. "One night only. Just to see you." He handed her one and sat. "My grandmother," he said, raising his glass, "was a special woman. Smart. Shrewd. She believed in tough love. And she had this way of always surprising me, keeping me on my toes, even from beyond the grave. I wish she were still here, that we could go back in time and speak to her once again. But since that's not possible, let's remember her. How formidable she was. To Linda Hughes."

"To Linda."

They clinked their glasses together, and she took a deep drink of the wine.

HOLDEN PINCHED THE bridge of his nose, not liking the ultimate outcome any more than Ashley.

"What do you mean we're releasing Todd?" she asked.

"We have no choice," he said, loathing the words.

"He aided and abetted his brother. He's complicit in murder."

Holden nodded. "But after conferring with his lawyer, Kyle has changed his story."

"You mean after being coerced by Todd's lawyer."

"Mr. Friedman is now also representing Kyle, who he claims is confused, delusional and in need of psychiatric treatment."

"Oh, please," Ashley scoffed. "Do you really believe that Kyle hallucinated seeing his brother and smashed his own hand with a hammer?"

"No." Holden sighed, hating the fact that Todd was going to walk. Yet again. "We have Emma's murderer. We have to accept the viable win and work on getting Todd another day." Although it sickened him to do it.

Ashley grabbed her jacket and threw on her cowboy hat. "I need some air." She stormed out of the office.

He understood her pain and his heart went out to her. But it wasn't in the cards for them to get Todd Burk today.

Melanie, who was still there, came over to him. "I saw the forensics reports, eliminating Jared Simpson's and Todd Burk's motorcycles. But it looks as if we'll get a match on the one Kyle was driving that night."

Holden nodded. "I only wish we could've nailed his brother as well."

"It's no secret that you want to see Todd go down for the crimes he's committed. I must admit that I'm surprised you handled this situation so objectively. He threw out tempting bait with his confession. If you had gone for it, you would've set up both our offices for an embarrassing fall when the case later crumbled, and he got a mistrial. I'll be sure to put in a good word on your behalf with the sheriff when he gets back."

It was nice to hear. "Thank you, but that's not necessary."

"Yes. It is. I only wish I could print up flyers about it and pass them around town for you. You deserve to be recognized after everything that happened. This was good work."

"Only doing my job."

"Merry Christmas." Melanie headed out.

Holden was ready to see Grace and give her an early Christmas present—the letter from Rodney Owens that Holden had tucked inside his inner jacket pocket. "Mitch, I'm going to head out a little early."

"Sure." The phone rang and he answered it. Just as Holden reached the door, Mitch said, "Hey, Holden, it's for you. It's your brother."

Whichever one it was should've waited until they were all at dinner together.

He traipsed back in and grabbed the phone. "This can't wait."

"Nope, it can't," Sawyer said.

"Then this better be good."

"Trust me, it is. We confirmed it was arson at Grace's place. And way more accelerant than necessary was used. That's why the place went up so quickly.

"From what I could tell, her smoke detectors were sabotaged. Not only that, but it wasn't only her bedroom room that had been nailed shut. All of them had been."

Holden's blood ran cold. "When I get my hands on whoever did it, heaven help them."

"You might get your wish. I checked out the emergency service log of 911 calls. Five total came in. Everyone identified themselves. Except for the first caller, who phoned in *ten minutes* earlier than the rest."

"Ten?" That was a long gap of time.

"Yup. Like maybe someone set that fire and at the last minute had a change of heart and called 911. That's not all, the second caller was Oscar Owens. Her neighbor."

"He owned the cottage."

"Oscar's niece was visiting at the time. They went outside to get a better look at the fire. He reported seeing a silver truck speeding down Old Mill away from the cottage, fishtailing all over the road. The niece got a partial license plate number and spotted a rental car placard around it."

Holden's pulse spiked. "Tell me you ran it."

"Who's your favorite brother?" Sawyer asked.

"You are, if you've got a name for me."

"I do. Traced the rental back to a Kevin Hughes from Los Angeles."

"Hughes?" This Kevin was her ex?

"You know the name."

"I do."

Oh my God.

That man had slashed her tires, run her off the road, set her house on fire while she was still inside. He'd been there in town for days, right across the street from Delgado's, all this time, watching her, stalking her.

Terrorizing her.

His gut burned with rage, then it was as if an icy fist clenched around his heart.

Grace. "I've got to go."

Chapter Nineteen

The room spun as Grace's vision blurred.

She set down the almost empty glass of wine, suddenly flushed and parched. "I better go. It's getting late."

Standing, she swayed. Everything around her tilted and whirled. She staggered forward and leaned back, bumping into the table. Pressing her palm to the smooth wood, she steadied herself. But the room still rocked from side to side, making her dizzy.

"Are you okay?" he asked.

"Um," she said, shaking her head to clear it. "Too much wine."

"Want me to get you some water?"

"No." Nausea rolled through her stomach. Her throat tightened. She was so thirsty. "I need to leave."

"Your coat is right there."

She stared across the room at it. Her coat seemed so far away. Everything became fuzzy, out of focus. Then her vision cleared. She took one step. And another.

Her knees turned to water as the floor seemed to shift under her feet and she collapsed onto the carpet.

Kevin rose from his seat and knelt over her. His expression transformed from affable and charming to predatory.

Dread twisted through her. "What did you do?" She reached up, swinging to hit his face, but she was too slow, her arm so heavy.

He easily pulled back out of her reach. "I laced your glass. Dosed the wine I gave you."

Panic spread through her as potent as whatever drug he'd used. "Why?"

"You're too good at defending yourself. I couldn't have you putting up a fight you might win. I needed you a little sedated, so that it'll be easier for me to do what comes next. I truly am sorry. But I have no other choice."

Those crazily familiar eyes she had stared into so many times in the past watched her closely. A surreal sense of horror washed through her.

"What?" Her voice was weak and shaky. "What are you talking about?"

"The wine is only part of what my grandmother left you." He took something out of his pocket. A piece of paper. He unfolded it and read it aloud. *"'Dearest Grace, you were an angel to me. You did more than care for me. You loved me and showed me kindness when I was at my weakest. To repay you, I wish to set you free, from your mother, from this job, which is stealing a piece of your soul because you're so sensitive. I bequeath you one million dollars. The rest of my money shall go to charity,'"* he said through clenched teeth. *"'Live a good a life free from financial worry.'"*

A tear leaked from her eye.

"She left *me* nothing!" He crumpled up the letter. "I contested it and lost. The only way I get anything is if you're dead and unable to receive it. Or we got married, but you said no. I bribed the executor to give me some time to *find you* myself."

"Kevin," she said, clutching his leg, needing him to see reason. It wasn't too late for him to stop this. "You can't. You wouldn't hurt me."

For all his faults, and there were many, he had never been violent.

"I didn't think I could, either," he said. "It wasn't my intention. Selene told me that you weren't happy here and you were being stubborn about coming back to California. I thought if I could nudge you, make things hard, scare you a little—cutting your tires, bumping you on the road, the fire—that you would be so happy and relieved to see me that you would jump at the prospect of marriage and going back home."

Her heart clenched. "That was you?" *Oh, God.* He had been sitting at the window, watching her and plotting. "You nearly killed me."

"I didn't mean to. The fire got so big, so fast. It just got beyond my control. Then I imagined you dead. That I had killed you. At first, it terrified me, and then I was relieved and surprisingly okay with it." His eyes took on a wild gleam. "I can live with your death on my hands."

She grabbed the bedspread and, grunting, tried to pull herself up, but she lacked the strength and flopped back to the floor. "Why?"

"I need the money," he gritted out. "My gambling debts have grown. I owe some ruthless people, really scary, dangerous people, a lot of money. This is my only option."

Desperation flooded her veins. "Kevin, please. You can have the money. I don't want it."

"If only I believed that you'd simply give it to me." He gave her a sad smile. "But I don't." He sat her up, slipped his arms around her torso from behind and hauled her body across the room.

She struggled and fought, digging in her heels, her feet skidding and failing to gain traction. Her efforts did nothing to slow him down. He dragged her through the bedroom to the bathroom. She reached out, grasping hold of the doorjamb, but he easily yanked her grip loose.

He threw her sluggish body to the floor and turned the water on in the bathtub. "I'll drown you here and toss your body in the river. I wish I could make it quick. Like a bullet to the head or something, but I need it to look like an accident."

Rolling onto her stomach, she crawled forward on her belly, using her forearms and elbows to pull herself. She didn't make it to the threshold before he snatched her by the hair and dragged her to the tub.

"Don't fight it." He brought his face close to hers and gave her a glacial stare. "It'll be faster, less painful for you, Grace, if you don't."

She thrust her head forward, opening her mouth, and bit down on his nose as hard as she could.

He screamed out in pain, and she clenched her teeth harder.

A metallic taste filled her mouth, and she knew it was

his blood. She couldn't punch him or shove him, but she did scratch him, digging her nails across his face to get as much of his DNA as she could under her nails.

He might kill her, but he wasn't going to get away with it.

Howling in agony, he punched her in the stomach, the blow sinking deep into her belly.

On a sharp exhale, she opened her mouth, releasing him. The shock was bad and the pain worse as it flared through her, stealing her breath. She wanted to gasp, to scream, to run, but she could do nothing, paralyzed by the fist he'd thrown.

Then he dunked her head into the water and held her under.

HOLDEN RUSHED INSIDE DELGADO'S, his gaze frantically sweeping the restaurant to find Grace.

But he didn't see her anywhere. Maybe she was in the kitchen, grabbing an order.

He hurried over to Xavier. "Where's Grace?"

Xavier shrugged. "She left."

"Left? Where did she go?"

"I don't know. Some guy I've never seen before showed up looking for her. They spoke at the bar and then she left with him."

Alarm streaked through him. He'd have to get an APB put out on the truck. That guy could've taken her anywhere. "How long ago did they leave?"

"Maybe ten or fifteen minutes. Why? Is everything all right?"

Holden tore out of Delgado's through the rear door

and dashed through the parking lot. He caught sight of the rental car—the silver pickup truck that had been damaged by the motorcycle Kyle was riding.

If the truck was still there, then it meant Kevin was inside and Grace was with him.

GRACE FLAILED, SUCKING IN a lungful of water, splashing more onto the floor. With one hand, she pushed up from the tub, and with the other, she reached back, smacking Kevin's face, hitting his nose.

He grunted in pain, his grip on her loosening just enough.

She shoved backward with all her might, breaking the surface. Coughing, spewing up water, she pushed up against the wall.

Growling, Kevin lunged for her. She thrust her foot out, tripping him. He couldn't regain his balance on the slippery floor and went crashing down onto the tile.

Grace wheezed as she gripped the toilet, fumbling to climb up. But her limbs were too weak. She couldn't move fast enough.

Kevin grabbed her, spinning her around, bringing them face-to-face. "Why won't you just die?" he screamed.

She hit him in the nose again, wishing she had the strength to do more.

He howled in agony. His features contorted in rage. He seized her throat with both his hands and shoved her backward.

She fell, her spine banging against the hard porcelain, her head smacking into the bottom of the tub.

He squeezed his hands, tightening his grip around

her throat, as he held her under the water. She kicked and clawed at his arms, desperate to pry them loose.

Through the water, she saw his face, the fury in his eyes, how he burned with determination, hell-bent on killing her.

Her lungs ached, burning with the need for oxygen. Thrashing, she wrestled against him, what little strength and energy she had draining from her.

She was drowning.

Air.

She needed air.

On a reflex, her mouth opened. She sucked water into her lungs and her body jerked to expel it. But he pressed harder, holding her down, keeping her locked under the water.

The light danced before her eyes. Darkness closed in on the edges of her vision.

She was going to die. It was probably over. But she refused to give up.

A loud crash sounded in the room.

Kevin's head swiveled toward the doorway.

A gunshot rang out like thunder. Once. Twice. The bullets threw Kevin backward, off her.

She shoved up, out of the water, raking in life-saving air. Spitting out water, she coughed.

"Grace!" Holden rushed to her, grabbing hold of her arms and hauling her out of the tub.

A strange, keening sound filled the room. Then she realized it was coming from her. She was weeping and wailing and shaking.

Putting a protective arm around her, he steered her

into the bedroom. But her legs gave way. He caught her, lifted her into his arms and set her down on the bed.

"K-Kevin," she sobbed, unable to calm down.

Holden closed the bathroom door, blocking the sight of the dead body. "I know," he said, sitting beside her. "Sawyer figured out that he set the fire and I came to find you."

"Again." She couldn't get the rest of the words out. He'd saved her life twice in two days.

Holden brought her into his arms and held her. "It's all right." He stroked her hair, kissed her forehead, whispering reassurances until she stopped shaking. "He's dead. Kevin can't hurt you anymore. No one is going to hurt you ever again." For several minutes, he rocked her. Then he pulled back and held her face in his hands. "We're meant to be together. To have this chance to love each other, to build a life, to have kids, to grow old together. Do you believe me?"

Looking into those clear blue eyes filled with so much love for her, she did. She could see it all. A life with him. Kids running around on the ranch. Long, lazy nights in bed with him. Laughing. Loving. Feeling safe.

"I believe you." She might not have believed in fate before, or even happily-ever-after, but without a doubt she knew they had earned it.

"Let's get you out of here and downstairs." He wrapped an arm around her as he helped her stand. At the door, he grabbed her coat and draped it across her shoulders and then carried her down the stairs. Once they reached the first floor, he pulled up a chair and sat her down. "While I call this in, I want you to do something for me."

"What?"

He knelt in front of her and pulled something from his jacket pocket. "Open your Christmas present."

A gift? Now? "I don't want anything." Everything she needed, she already had. Her life. An understanding with her mother. Holden. A chance at happiness.

"Aren't you curious?" He handed her an envelope.

"What is it?"

"A handwritten apology. From Rodney Owens."

She laughed through her tears. Somehow, someway, Holden had done it again, managing to uplift her in the darkest moments. And she knew that he would continue to do so for as long as they were together.

* * * * *

#2115 LAWMAN TO THE CORE
The Law in Lubbock County • by Delores Fossen
When an intruder attacks Hallie Stanton and tries to kidnap the baby she's adopting, her former boss, ATF agent Nick Brodie, is on the case. But will his feelings for Hallie and her son hinder his ability to shut down a dangerous black market baby ring?

#2116 DOCKSIDE DANGER
The Lost Girls • by Carol Ericson
To protect his latest discovery, FBI agent Tim Ruskin needs LAPD homicide detective Jane Falco off the case. But when intel from the FBI brass clashes with the clues Jane is uncovering, Tim's instincts tell him to put his trust in the determined cop, peril be damned.

#2117 MOUNTAIN TERROR
Eagle Mountain Search and Rescue • by Cindi Myers
A series of bombings have rocked Eagle Mountain, and Deni Traynor's missing father may be the culprit. SAR volunteer Ryan Welch will help the vulnerable schoolteacher unearth the truth. But will the partnership lead them to their target...or something more sinister?

#2118 BRICKELL AVENUE AMBUSH
South Beach Security • by Caridad Piñeiro
Mariela Hernandez has a target on her back, thanks to her abusive ex-husband's latest plot. Teaming up with Ricky Gonzalez and his family's private security firm is her only chance at survival. With bullets flying, Ricky will risk it all to be the hero Mariela needs.

#2119 DARK WATER DISAPPEARANCE
West Investigations • by K.D. Richards
Detective Terrence Sutton is desperate to locate his missing sister—one of three women who recently disappeared from Carling Lake. The only connection to the crimes? A run-down mansion and Nikki King, the woman Terrence loved years ago and who's now back in town...

#2120 WHAT IS HIDDEN
by Janice Kay Johnson
Jo Summerlin's job at her stepfather's spectacular limestone cavern is thrown into chaos when she and former navy SEAL Alan Burke discover a pile of bones and a screaming stranger. Have they infiltrated a serial killer's perfect hiding place?

Get 4 FREE REWARDS!

We'll send you 2 FREE Books plus 2 FREE Mystery Gifts.

FREE Value Over **$20**

Both the **Harlequin Intrigue®** and **Harlequin® Romantic Suspense** series feature compelling novels filled with heart-racing action-packed romance that will keep you on the edge of your seat.

YES! Please send me 2 FREE novels from the Harlequin Intrigue or Harlequin Romantic Suspense series and my 2 FREE gifts (gifts are worth about $10 retail). After receiving them, if I don't wish to receive any more books, I can return the shipping statement marked "cancel." If I don't cancel, I will receive 6 brand-new Harlequin Intrigue Larger-Print books every month and be billed just $6.24 each in the U.S. or $6.74 each in Canada, a savings of at least 14% off the cover price or 4 brand-new Harlequin Romantic Suspense books every month and be billed just $5.24 each in the U.S. or $5.99 each in Canada, a savings of at least 13% off the cover price. It's quite a bargain! Shipping and handling is just 50¢ per book in the U.S. and $1.25 per book in Canada.* I understand that accepting the 2 free books and gifts places me under no obligation to buy anything. I can always return a shipment and cancel at any time by calling the number below. The free books and gifts are mine to keep no matter what I decide.

Choose one: ☐ **Harlequin Intrigue Larger-Print** (199/399 HDN GRA2) ☐ **Harlequin Romantic Suspense** (240/340 HDN GRCE)

Name (please print)

Address _____ Apt. #

City _____ State/Province _____ Zip/Postal Code

Email: Please check this box ☐ if you would like to receive newsletters and promotional emails from Harlequin Enterprises ULC and its affiliates. You can unsubscribe anytime.

Mail to the **Harlequin Reader Service:**
IN U.S.A.: P.O. Box 1341, Buffalo, NY 14240-8531
IN CANADA: P.O. Box 603, Fort Erie, Ontario L2A 5X3

Want to try 2 free books from another series! Call 1-800-873-8635 or visit www.ReaderService.com.

HARLEQUIN
PLUS

Announcing a **BRAND-NEW**
multimedia subscription service
for romance fans like you!

Read, Watch and Play.

Experience the easiest way to get
the romance content you crave.

Start your **FREE 7 DAY TRIAL** at
<u>www.harlequinplus.com/freetrial</u>.